Advance Praise for *Wh*

"Sue Borgersen's mini-fictions are lik   ͜ ͜ peek through a neighbour's window. You glance with curiosity then quickly move on. However, the image stays etched in your mind. You think about what you have just read and want to connect the images to understand, to know. These poetic mini-fictions flow fast from story to story and are carefully-crafted windows that lead the reader to fondly wonder."

—**J.J. Lokshtanov** (Jack). Montreal poet, journalist, editor.

"Witty and insightful, many of Sue Borgersen's tiny stories appeared on the weekly *Ad Hoc Fiction* ebook since 2016 and have inspired other writers from all over the world."

—**Jude Higgins**, writer, writing tutor, events organiser at Bath Flash Fiction.

"I'm a great fan of Sue Borgersen's imaginative and inventive writing. The warmth and humanity shine through her stories."

—**Vanessa Couchman**, author of the *Tales of Corsica* series.

While the Kettle Boils

Micro fiction

by

S.B. Borgersen

Attention schools and businesses: for discounted copies on large orders, please contact the publisher directly.

For information contact:
Unsolicited Press
Portland, Oregon
www.unsolicitedpress.com
orders@unsolicitedpress.com
619-354-8005

Cover Design: Kathryn Gerhardt
Editor: S.R. Stewart

ISBN: 978-1-950730-74-2

For my mother, Pauline,
who taught me to love a good story

Author's Note

When I set out to write this author's note, I instinctively wanted to tell you my story. Of my lifetime of experiences, of living on islands around the world (on both sides of the equator), and of all the curious, lovable, and on occasion, wicked characters that have crossed my path.

Instead I'll let these minute fictions tell those stories for me. I couldn't have written them without living in those places, pinching morsels of those characters, or without feeling those feelings.

These stories were often drafted without conscious thought. They span three years of writing but pull on a lifetime of living.

S.B. Borgersen

Contents

While the Kettle Boils

Micro fiction

1. Gerald Gave Her Slippers

Sylvia pulls at the loose thread, watching her sleeve slowly unravel. The kingfisher blue wool collects in unruly tiny loops. It curls on the floor, pooling in a wriggling mess beside her red plaid bedroom slippers, the ones someone gave her. She touches the slippers with her toes; nudging them away from the pile of endless blue worms.

When did she get the slippers? It had to be for her birthday. Which birthday? Or was it Christmas? It was Gerald. Wasn't it?

But didn't Gerald hate Christmas? "A load of commercial clap-trap," he always said. She could hear his stern voice still. She could see him. With a sneer, opening the gift she'd carefully made for him. Ripping off the wrapping paper printed with laughing Santas. Always the same gift. Hand-knitted grey merino socks: To Gerald, love forever, Sylvia.

She pulls at more loose threads. The sleeve of her cardigan disappears as spirals of curling wool grow at her feet. She examines her exposed fragile arm with its paper-thin skin, touches the collection of brown spots her kind doctor diagnosed as 'wisdom marks.'

And Sylvia remembers.

It was her birthday. The family get-together at the Lotus Garden. Her cake with ninety candles. Gerald gave her the ugly red plaid slippers with pom-poms, in a shoebox. With a stick-on silver bow.

And she wore her newly knitted cardigan in kingfisher blue.

2. How to Lose Your Leg—A Step by Step Guide

It's only a scratch, they say, just dab it with TCP.

The TCP is pretty acrid, I give that a swerve, you know me.

It's night, scratching the itch, my leg raging hot, I resort to Johnny Walker and drop into a welcome stupor.

Dawn breaks. Shaking like I've got hippy-hippy shakes, I make it to Outpatients. Wait for hours before a soundless TV. I vomit over the waiting room floor. You know me. That gets attention.

They roll up the leg of my jeans. Violet blisters the size of my fist that weren't there this morning. Were they? I fade away. Not like me; I'm more your Buddy Holly kinda guy. Aren't I?

Necrotizing fasciitis is on the chart hanging at the foot of my hospital bed. Nil by Mouth hangs over my head.

Amputation, the only solution, they say.

Now I have an itch I cannot scratch.

3. Multidimensional Big Talk

Billy knew it wouldn't take much to crash the systems; it was a simple contiguous network. He'd watched Jonathon design the pilot project. Provided answers whenever Jonathon asked. As he'd done since they were best buddies at Middle School.

He witnessed Jonathon, puffed up like a blowfish, presenting to the board. Explaining how the mesh of multidimensional latticing would save the corporation big money. How it would reduce staff tenfold and how that alone would justify the multimillion dollar spend. Reducing overheads and creating a swift and smooth flow of time-critical information through the company would make business soar.

That's why Billy's Alyson was laid off. And why she had gone downhill so fast. Why she had lost the baby, their baby. And why their future looked bleak.

"I'll give him 'mesh of multidimensional' big talk," muttered Billy, snipping the single vulnerable cable that made it all work.

4. The Eclipse

The sun cracks the horizon like a vermillion scimitar. "We'll never see the likes of this again," says Robert, his arm clamped across Sheila's shoulders.

She pushes away his ownership of her. His dictatorship. Eating dull food. Wearing drab clothes. Staying in. Everything done at his bidding.

He pulls her towards him. "Listen."

"I can't hear a thing. The birds have stopped singing, even the sea is still."

"Precisely," he says, "we are alone, the sun is eclipsing. No-one to hear or see you either."

***

At his wake, a Mexican Ranchera band yells, "El Grito Mexicano."

Sheila enters wearing a yellow halter neck top and tight white jeans. She sashays to the buffet table, slices into a large blood orange, knowing he would have hated it. She sucks the orange.

The sharp red juices trickle down her neck to her breasts. She smiles in remembrance of his death rattle.

5. Now That's Panache

'The Lancaster is 70 feet long with a wingspan of 102 feet,' she announces with panache.

Panache?

I drag my tablet from my pocket. Google panache: something to do with feathers—French origin. Sounds about right; she is a tad fluffy. Her hair all golden feathers. She's babbling about speeds of 275 mph and ceilings of 25,600 feet. But wait.

Did I hear her say 'float'?

She did. I know she did. And I quote: 'The Lancaster bomber, with four 1,640 horsepower Merlin engines could float above the clouds.'

Merlins roar. Float is the last image that comes to mind. Who's she kidding? I'd like to see her up there with that deafening din going on. Floating. Light as a feather no doubt.

Later, over a glass or more of wine, I zip up my flying jacket and ask her. "Have you been up in one?"

6. Packed Lunch

"Not meat paste again," he growls. "Have you any idea what's in that crap?"

Marcia looks at Steve: at his thuggish hands grasping the sandwich bag, at the white bread with the anaemic pink stripe between the slices, not unlike his pasty face with his gash of a pink mouth yelling.

"What the hell happens to the money I give you for my food?"

She tries a smile, "It's home-made," she says, "slowly simmered best steak finely ground with the spices you love. You couldn't possibly take a steak with you on the train. This is better."

Marcia watches Steve: down the garden path, through the gate, his brutish head bouncing as he marches up the lane to Station Road.

In the afternoon she waits, anticipating the doorbell, the police, gently telling her, "You'd better sit down. It's your husband. He's been found dead on the Birmingham train."

7. The Roar of Repetition

There was a hint of a catch in his voice: goodbye Sarah. He climbed onto his bike and within minutes became a distant roar.

Sarah stayed motionless. She already regretted not saying: goodbye Michael. Wished she had not pleaded: don't go. Nor begged: please stay; don't leave me.

She heard the roar in her head for days.

Weeks later Sarah senses the roar returning. Getting louder. Stopping beneath her window. Michael dismounting the gleaming black beast. His leathers coated with ash grey dust. His tired face attempting a smile. Of remorse?

She can hear her voice breaking the silence: I'm so relieved you're back. Saying: I've missed you so much. Imploring: please don't leave me again. Finally: I love you.

But she won't. She knows Michael would climb back on the Harley and roar off and out of her clinging clutches.

8. Skim

"Remember. Scum always rises," Mick said. "Then we'll skim it off the top."

Kat crouched between the tall pines—Mick's orders. Smart Mick who'd been to uni. Who'd found her last year. Who'd shown her she wasn't scum.

Mick pulled at his NY ball cap. The sign for Kat to do what she still did best. With innate stealth she threaded her way to the hill. Thankful to be the hunter. No longer the hunted.

She heard them before she saw them. Loud. In the clearing. Huddled. Bottles of hard liquor at their lips. A familiar haze over their heads.

"Hey," she called.

"Huh. That you Tiger-Kat? Where ya bin?"

"Got ya something," she said before slinking back into the undergrowth. She climbed the hill trail. Weaving. Stopping. Listening. Knowing they were following.

Knowing Mick would be waiting at the top.

9. Three's Company

"It's time to branch out," she says. "Time to diversify. Bring Alex on board with new ideas."

Jim twists his face. "Alex? Why Alex? You're still in love with him. Aren't you?"

Gina feels her face flush, feels her earlobes burn, feels—well—just feels, for the first time in months. There's a stirring in her belly. "Nothing like that," she says. "I just think he could move us forward and get us out of this hole."

The partnership with Jim had seemed such a great idea. A chance for her design skills to flourish. An outlet for her talent. His practical and experienced approach to business was exactly what she needed.

Giving up Alex - with his dreams, his ideals and extraordinary ideas, with plans that would never work—was not a good idea Gina tells herself now.

But this could be perfect. Like having cake and eating it too.

10. There's the Rub

There's a friendly friction between Danny and Rick. Always has been. Right from Gilbert Street School when they both wanted the same black wax crayon. When they resolved the conflict by cutting it in half with Rick's penknife. An exact half—it was measured with a precision they became renowned for.

Later, they shared a bike, with Rick using the black Raleigh with dropped handlebars on Mondays, Wednesdays, and Saturdays. And Danny on Sundays, Tuesdays, and Fridays. Thursdays it got its wash and polish, chrome cleaned, and chain oiled. Both lads sharing the chore, chatting as they went. Over a few illicit cans.

When they were eighteen they saved and bought the baby blue Reliant Robin, keeping the same schedule. Of course, there were days when they went out together, two lads, having fun, chatting up the girls. Like well-oiled pistons.

Then along comes Doreen.

11. Lady in Red

She wears Valentino red. Her model face shows no emotion. Except her unforgettable violet eyes, scanning the room.

The air hangs as she enters. The gabble-talk hum stops. She descends the wide staircase. Her hand, in a black, elbow-length glove, snakes its way down the golden handrail like an elegant caterpillar. Her feet, unseen beneath folds of red silk, make no sound on the marble.

She crosses the hall to Jasper. All heads turn.

She is at his side.

"Giselle," he says. "You came."

"Hush," she says, arresting his single tear with a fingertip of her glove.

12. The Choker

Bernie knits. The rhythm provides her with a form of meditation. While she knits she sorts out world problems. And others closer to home. Specifically the bitch Veronica.

She has taken to knitting necklaces with wire. Fine 32-gauge silver wire. Bernie ordered it online; it arrived last month along with size 0 bamboo double-ended needles.

The clever leaf design is worked out on graph paper. Beginning with just four stitches, she carefully winds the wire tightly around her finger. She pulls it even tighter around the needle, imagining the finished choker.

With each row she increases until there are 24 stitches, the halfway point. Bernie's pulse races as she begins the decrease until the fine filigree neck piece is complete and the gilt clasp is woven into place.

All that remains now is to give it to Veronica and offer to fasten it for her. Securely.

13. The Pact

The pink lipstick stain on the cup is the only sign that Sylvie was ever here.

The coffee dregs are at least a week old. Encrusted at the bottom. Last Wednesday's Telegraph crossword half completed. Then I see Jubilee, dear Golden Jubilee, peacefully laid out like a snow angel in the bottom of her canary cage. Sylvie would never leave Jube.

I slump in the chintz covered wing chair, consider making myself coffee but know the milk will be soured. Where is Sylvie? Has she got our agreement confused? Or is it me?

We had a pact, Sylvie and me, that we would travel this dead-end road together. I reach into my pocket for my diary. Indeed, we'd agreed on Wednesday. And today is Wednesday. The 27th.

I look up at Sylvie's wall calendar. There is a red circle around the 20th.

14. The Cake

Rob wasn't home. It didn't bother Sally; he often went off in search of a unique ingredient. She started without him, beating eggs, sugar, butter. Adding flour. Tasting. It needed a pinch of something more. Cinnamon? Ginger? Nutmeg?

She scanned the rows of exotic spices on Rob's shelves. Opened some, sniffed, dipped in her finger. Tasted.

There was something about the scarlet powder that enthralled her. It would turn the cake an amazing colour, she told herself. There was no label, but she was sure Rob had all the best ingredients; he was a famous cake baker.

The cake took pride of place in the bake sale. And was immediately snapped up at $10.

The news of Rob's arrest, for poisoning his producer with a cake, had the village in shock. And Sally rushing around to find out who had bought her cake before it was too late.

15. Smoke Gets in Your Eyes

She is just a wisp of a girl. And he, a giant among men.

They walk hand in hand through the streets of Famagusta during the Orange Festival. From a distance you'd think they were father and daughter. But they stop by the fountain. Kiss. And stroll slowly on. Talking. Listening. His head bowed low to hear her.

In the empty bar of the King George Hotel he plays Smoke Gets in Your Eyes for her. His over-large fingers floating over the piano keys with a lightness you would not expect.

It is the moment they fall in love. And will be their single lasting memory.

With this sudden shift in their chemistry they leave their half-finished brandy sours on the bar, remove their shoes on the steps of the hotel, head down to the beach, and into the night.

16. Crofters' Stones

They find the crofters' coastal cemetery and park at the entrance; a gap between two stone walls. Overgrown, neglected. Out of the car they are besieged by clouds of infamous Highland midges. Undeterred and protected by their Canadian bug jackets they continue in their quest to find the graves of their Scottish ancestors.

There are no marked graves. Mother and daughter look at each other and scan the cemetery. All they see are rough round stones, the size of footballs. No names, nor dates, no RIPs. Walking between the rows, they notice subtle differences between the stones. And wonder.

The white sands of Berneray meet the edge of the cemetery. Snipes drum and corncrakes rasp. Wading birds come into view: sanderlings and curlews and herons.

As they watch the gannets dive, mother and daughter turn to each other knowing that they have found their ancestors.

17. Regret

Her party dress: pink with butterflies and sequins, set off with a large bow, the ribbon ends floated behind her when she moved.

Her tiny pumps: pale violet with fine satin ribbons crisscrossing over and up the ankles, finishing with an elegant bow and allowing the satin ribbons to swirl around when she pirouetted. Her pirouettes so swift the ribbons become a blur of violet, like rapid dragonfly wings over summer ponds.

Her hair: fair and fine as gossamer, scooped in a French twist and held in place by a glittering diamanté clip. The sparkle in her eyes exceeding those of the clip.

That is how I will always remember her. Eighty years ago. Beautiful, gentle, kind.

When life got in the way we lost touch. I finger the letter from her granddaughter, bearing the sad news, and allow a tear of regret to fall.

18. Water but No Wine

It is a steep climb to the monastery at Mount Stavrovouni. We use twisting goat paths to ease our way. They double the distance but are easier than a vertical ascent. Wild thyme and garlic grow abundantly between the loose rocks; the pungent mix of herbal scents fills the air.

"Time for another song," calls Jim, our leader, and the group bursts into a hearty but breathy rendering of Climb Climb Up Sunshine Mountain (heavenly breezes blow).

I wish a breeze would indeed blow; the Cyprus sun beats down and I pray for an ice-cold beer at the top.

We make it to the monastery and are greeted by a Greek priest who offers us cold water for our dusty feet before we, in turn, kiss the glass of the frame protecting a splinter of The Cross.

But there's no sign of beer. Nor wine.

19. Speed Bonnie Boat

The sky was a slate canopy as she boarded the flight. She'd really wanted to approach the islands slowly. By boat to Lochmaddy from Skye. 'Speed bonnie boat like a bird...' playing in her head full of Flora MacDonald and Bonnie Prince Charlie.

Like the way she'd approached Symi years before. Churning diesel motors throbbing across the Aegean from Rhodes, passing the famous Colossus, into azure seas. A balalaika playing. Three slow hours of blinding blue skies until the island, with its russet roofed ochre dwellings, came into view. Some hollow shells; reminders of war.

The descent into Benbecula was too soon. There had been nothing but clouds as they'd left Glasgow and flown over Oban. But now she could look down on the treeless harshness of the Outer Hebrides. Then the gentle white sands kissed by the sea. The islands of her ancestors.

Everything now made perfect sense.

20. Martin

He was a tiny mite. Like a china doll. Fliss found him behind the bus station; took him back to the squat. Her fellow squatters were still asleep. The baby screamed, red in the tiny face. Jag stretched and got up. No-one else stirred.

"Fliss, hang him in this net bag, it's my hunting scale, looks like he's maybe a preemie," Jag said.

"4 lbs 2 oz." she read. "OMG Baby, we need to find you something to eat." She reached for the box of KD.

Jag shook his head and warmed milk on the Primus. He dipped his pinky finger into the milk and gently put it against the baby's rosebud mouth. The crying stopped, the baby snuffled and began to suckle.

Fliss didn't wonder why Jag knew this stuff. But she loved him for it.

"Can we keep him?" she said. "I will call him Martin."

21. Choice

"You must pick," Jenny said. "Annabelle or me."

Richard was torn. He loved Jenny for her big blue eyes, her long wavy fair hair, her shapely tanned legs, and her wicked smile. She also had rich parents.

But he loved Annabelle too. She wasn't a looker, but there was something that awoke in Richard a completely new feeling; that of admiration. Annabelle wore charity shop clothes, worked a weekend job, and her dark hair she cut herself in a short pixie mop.

Richard knew Annabelle was smart too, a thinker.

This was his dilemma. Beauty over brains. He decided to let the girls make the decision for him. He thought himself a bit on the brainy side too. He gave them each the same question.

And they each gave the same reply. Then walked away. Arm in arm.

22. Not Mimi

There was a flow to his speech, a lyrical quality. He said he was from The Valley, as if that explained everything. His name was Merle Minstrel.

And that is what she loved. For she lived for music. The fact that his anger bubbled up like a Rodolpho aria in La Bohème softened the blows somewhat.

His apologies always came in the form of three dozen yellow rosebuds. Tied with royal blue silk muslin. As he gave them to her on bended knee he sang.

It was her daughter Vanessa who pointed out that life wasn't just about music. That she could buy that from iTunes if it was that flipping important.

And yellow rosebuds didn't really go with black eyes too well anyway.

23. Dancers

"Come trip the light fantastic with me," he said.

"I'll need more than your sweet talk to persuade me," she replied.

"A cruise then, the Med, c'mon Brenda."

She didn't take much more persuading and before the summer was over, they were floating around the Greek Islands waltzing and foxtrotting at every stop. Brenda in her silver dancing shoes and off-the-shoulder gowns. He in his patent leathers, bowties, and tuxedo. They did indeed cut a fine couple.

When Jed twisted his ankle climbing to the remains of The Lionheart's castle on the island of Symi it threw them for a loop. "What'll we do Brend?" he wailed, sitting under the vine canopy at the outdoor bar sipping a cold Mythos beer.

"Like you, I'll just have to soldier on, Jed," she said, looking in the direction of Andreas, who just that morning had taught her to Zorba.

24. Once in a Blue Moon

Melissa was in a bit of a bind, a kind of heartbreak situation with Nick.

But she couldn't get hold of her mother, Brenda, who was dancing her way around the Greek Islands with some guy named Jed. All Melissa wanted was a hug, the warmth of her mother's bosom.

She called her old friend Abby, "Nick's a brute," she said.

"I told you so, weeks ago." said Abby. "You do pick 'em. D'ya fancy clubbing tonight then, Mel?"

They hadn't been to The Blue Moon for at least a year; it wasn't where Melissa met Nick, that, at least, was a comfort.

Melissa and Abby danced around their handbags for a few dances. Back in their dimmed booth, after sips of vodka coolers, their hands reached and fingertips touched, they looked into each other's mascara lined eyes, leaned across the table and kissed.

25. Missed the Boat?

Jed was quite at home under the vine covered awning with kebabs and a bottle of Aphrodite, his injured ankle having been gently massaged by Maria.

His dancing partner, Brenda, was nowhere in sight. He watched the cruise ship leave the harbour and felt no regrets that he'd missed the boat. He didn't miss Brenda either.

"I've reached a turning point in my life," he told Maria.

"Δεν έχει σημασία—it doesn't matter," she replied, nodding.

Jed looked directly at her, noticing, for the first time, a gentle fold in the fine tawny skin of her neck. Right where her gold chain rested. He noticed her deep brown eyes, the colour of chestnuts, and how they smiled. He took another sip of the iced fruity wine and, as Maria bustled off to collect another tasty morsel from the kitchen for him, he hoped his ankle wouldn't heal too swiftly.

26. Brenda's Decision

Brenda sat on the dockside watching the fit fishermen, Andreas in particular. She watched his bronzed muscles ripple as he beat the purple dye from the octopuses he'd caught in his net in the early hours of that morning.

She remembered waking between the rumpled cotton sheets to find a hollow beside her and smiled at the memory of the night before.

Brenda looked up from watching the mesmerizing scene of busy fishermen to see her cruise ship leave the harbour with a couple of toots of its horn. She gave herself an imaginary pat on the back for making the decision not to go. She wondered, briefly, if Jed was worried she wasn't on board beside him.

She waved at Andreas and indicated with her thumb and pinkie finger that she was going to make a phone call; it was time to let her daughter Melissa know.

27. Mel and Abby

Melissa heard her phone. But she was right there in the absolute middle of trying to get a splinter out of the fourth finger on her right hand.

"Let it ring, Mel," said Abby. "My boss always says if it's important, they'll ring again. Here, let me look."

"It could be Mum you know," said Melissa, "she's due home next Tuesday, you'll have to move out."

"Hmmm, what'll we tell her?" said Abby, "has she got any kind of clue about... about...?"

"God no, she'll freak for a bit, but she's open minded. I think."

"Gottit," yelled Abby holding the splinter aloft between pink tweezers.

Melissa smiled. But there was a lump in her throat. She imagined Brenda walking in through the front door, tanned from dancing around Greek Islands, saying, "Well, have you patched things up with Nick, Melly?"

And Mel wished she could say, "Yes, Mum."

28. Missing?

Brenda was worried. Her daughter wasn't answering. She usually had her mobile phone glued to her hand. Or ear. Was she an irresponsible mother to leave her home alone and go off dancing around the Greek islands?

She sat on the balcony of her new lover's apartment with a glass of wine and looked across the bay, at the clusters of red roofed, straw coloured houses. And at the skeletons of houses that were destroyed in the war. She couldn't imagine what that was like for the islanders and she wasn't prepared to ask Andreas what his gentle grandmother felt. But she wondered, why keep these ruins as constant reminders?

Brenda was deep in thought, still asking herself questions, when her phone rang. Startled, and yet relieved, she answered "Where've you been?"

But it wasn't her daughter. It was the cruise ship office asking her the same question.

29. New Partner

Jed drifted away on Maria's balcony. He dreamt of a full English breakfast with sausages, mushrooms, and crisp grilled bacon. His mouth watered. He could smell it. Taste it even.

A soft nudge of his elbow; it was Maria in a blue sleeveless dress, smiling.

"Our breakfasts. We eat together," she said, her English improving. She set down the tray on the glass topped wicker table. Jed looked at the thick pottery bowls of fresh yoghurt and honey. A glass dish of almonds on the side. A pot of steaming strong dark coffee.

Jed closed his eyes again and wondered how Brenda might be getting on without him. If she was tucking into her full English with a pot of Orange Pekoe. And if she'd been able to continue dancing without him.

"Maria," he said, taking her slim hand in his, "do you dance?"

30. Body Language

Brenda watched Andreas flex his muscles. He grunted, hauling fish boxes to the dockside. She caught his eye. He gave her a single large wave. The kind that meant something.

Waving hands plus head nodding was another language for Brenda to learn. She knew that a single up-nod with a 'tuh' meant 'no.' That Andreas' mother playfully swatting her giant of a son with a blue checkered tea towel, accompanied by, 'Ο Θεός μου είναι ένας ηλίθιος,' meant 'oh my God you are an idiot.'

Then Andreas scooping up his light-as-a-sparrow mother and swinging her around until they both laughed so much he had to stop.

Brenda loved to see such feeling between mother and son; it was a new experience for her. She was reminded of the old-wives' tale: if you want to know how a man will treat you, watch how he treats his mother.

31. Decision Dilemma

Abby is in bed with 'flu. Mel coddles her with Lemsip, toast, and, once she'd found the perished pink hot water bottle at the back of the airing cupboard, filled it (with her fingers crossed it wouldn't leak), tucked her BFF in with a 'hope you feel better soon,' retreats to the kitchen with a beer.

'Mum where are you?' she can't get out the question of her head. Mel hasn't heard from her mother in over a week; should she phone the cruise ship company? Then, 'how can I get Abby to leave when she is so poorly?' comes next.

Her concerns are intertwined; one cannot release the other. She scratches her head. Watches flake after flake of dandruff float down into her beer glass like a gentle snowfall over her mother's garden pond.

Mel decides. In the shower with the Head & Shoulders she changes her mind. Again.

32. A Night to Remember

Maria takes time to prepare, coils her long wavy deep brown hair, weaves in sprigs of sweet-smelling jasmine. She wears drifting, deep blue muslin. White sandals on her tanned feet. Pink painted toenails.

Jed thinks she is a picture of beauty. He tells her.

Maria doesn't blush but dips her head coyly. Smiles the smile Jed loves and says, "And you." She takes him by the hand and leads him down the track to the village.

The village dance is not what Jed expects. Not traditional, not classical, just people bobbing up and down to well-worn pop music.

By midnight the dance settles into couples shuffling in each other's arms.

Jed calls to the villagers, "Can anyone do the twist?"

The band erupts into Twist and Shout. Maria kicks off her sandals. She and Jed lead the village dancers into a night to remember.

33. Good Vibrations

"Tonight. We go out," says Andreas, running his damp fingers down Brenda's neck.

Brenda languishes with a Mills and Boon on the verandah. Andreas glistens, fresh from the shower. With a large primrose towel wrapped around his waist, he reminds Brenda of the latest Oikos yoghurt advert on TV back home.

"Hmmm," she says, "was hoping we could stay home…"

"There are plenty of nights for us," he says, ignoring Brenda's twinkling eyes and fluttering eyelashes, "but tonight is special, I have two tickets for the band."

Brenda hauls herself up from her languishing. "Band?" she says, "what band?"

"I have two tickets for The Beach Boys, they are here for just one night before they go to Istanbul."

Brenda leaps from her recliner, hugs Andreas like he's never been hugged, and begins to sing, "I'm pickin' up good vibrations…"

34. Return to the Moon

Mel and Abby haven't been to The Blue Moon in a dog's age. Going again was Abby's idea.

"I'm taking you out tonight," she said.

"Me?" said Mel. "Tonight? What shall I wear?"

It isn't as they remember. The memories of their first kiss have been waning for some time, at least on Mel's part. But they sit close, in their old booth, drinking vodka coolers and, from time to time, shuffling (to old Barry White records) around the tiny, round dance floor in each other's arms.

For Mel, the spark has gone. She cannot bring herself to speak, let alone tell Abby how she feels. They steer themselves around a clutch of giggling girls who dance around a heap of bright pink and purple handbags.

"Let's go home." says Abby.

Mel realises that Abby now has her feet well under the table. She shivers.

35. Floating Mansions

Brenda gazes, open mouthed, at the sight below in the harbour. A flotilla of luxury yachts has arrived overnight. They are moored, daisy-chain style, along the waterfront.

Andreas is not with her, she can only assume he was called out to help, as he often does with customs and immigration formalities.

She eats the still-warm chocolate croissant Andreas has thoughtfully left for her, sinks her teeth into the ripe peach beside it, letting the sweet juices trickle down her chin, savours the thick black coffee, showers, pulls on her white shorts and turquoise t-shirt, and heads down to the harbour.

The yachts are huge; floating mansions dancing gently side-by-side. Brenda stops before the largest: The Spray, Halifax Nova Scotia. There on the forward deck sipping cocktails at eight in the morning with a slim brunette is Jed. And Andreas. Laughing.

36. Buck's Fizz

Jed puts down his Buck's Fizz and reaches for Maria's slim brown hand. He strokes her fingers heavy with gold. Then looks back, open mouthed, at the quayside where Brenda stands, also open mouthed.

Maria says, "What is the matter Gerald?"

Brenda laughs then, "Gerald is it?" she says. "Gone up in the world have we Jed? Landed yourself a nice piece of floating luxury then?"

Jed cannot reply, he cannot get the words out. His face turns purple. Andreas, with his usual concern urges Jed to sit down, "Please," he says, "stay calm, drink this," and offers him a tall glass of iced water.

"I think we need a doctor," says Maria, "this is not the first time this has happened."

37. New Perspective

'To hell with it,' says Mel to the empty space where Abby would sit, 'I'm going to have a bath.'

She needs to think about the postcard from Greece. And the fact that it bears a French stamp. Mel does all her best thinking in the bath.

She breathes deeply. The rose geranium bath oils seeps into her limbs, her joints, her mind.

It is the first time she's felt immense liberation since her mother left for the Greek Islands; since she disappeared without much more than a couple of calls and a text message, since she, Mel, rejected Nick, rejected Abby.

The postcard is her corner to turn. She will not question the French stamp. She will not hang around and wait for others to get her life to restart.

She slowly lowers herself beneath the sweet-smelling oils and sees her world from a new perspective.

38. Honey

Brenda sits at Jed's bedside in the Greek hospital. It is just before dawn and Brenda has thought long and hard about what the heck the pair of them are playing at.

She gently spoons honey from the jar on her lap into the glass of tea. As she stirs the clear golden honey into the steaming amber tea she is careful not to let the spoon chink against the glass. Careful not to wake Jed.

He is sleeping normally now; the anxiety she felt when he collapsed is now over. She breathes deeply with each stir of the spoon. She will not wake him to let him sip the tea but brings it to her own lips. She tastes Greece. She smells the summer. She hears the gentle lap of waves upon the shore.

And she knows it is time to take Jed home.

39. When you're not strong

Some…times in our lives…Brenda sings in her head.

She gently places her left foot behind her and her right forward. She imagines she is dancing with Jed. She swallows hard. Breakfast tastes like cardboard. Gone is the fragrance of honey and peaches, of almonds and yoghurt. The island sun has sapped her senses.

We all have pain… she feels Jed's pain, his leg, and now his stroke. And the sadness written on his tanned face …we all have sorrow…

She stops to take a sip of cold beer and looks out at the harbour. At the fishermen beating squid, hearing the thump of each beating but…if we are wise…

Andreas waves, she sees but ignores him,…there's always tomorrow…

Then she lets it rip, lean on me, when you're not strong…

I'll be your friend, somebody to lean on…

Then bursts into tears.

40. Cold Feet

Mel steps out of the bath onto the icy, marble tiled floor. "Shit," she says, "where's the bathmat?"

She reaches for a towel, one of the big fluffy cream bath sheets her mother keeps folded on the rack, always handy, always in good supply. The rack is empty. "Shit," she says again.

Mel is alone now, Abby left without a by-your-leave and Mel's mother is bobbing around somewhere in the Mediterranean with her dandy boyfriend.

She wraps her towelling dressing gown around her, slouches to the kitchen and fills the kettle for a cuppa. Tea seems to be the answer for Mel now, "Am I getting old?" she wails. "Is this what it's come to?"

When the phone rings Mel jumps, it is her mother. Mel wants to scream with rage, 'Where've you been, you cow?'

Instead, she says, "Please come home, Mum. Please."

41. The Return

Nick finds Mel zonked out on the chintzy Ikea sofa. Three empty beer bottles on the floor. Empty pill packets alongside.

He taps her on each cheek, and, getting no response, gives her a good shake.

"You?" she says, her voice quivering like a copse of spring poplars in a light breeze. "How the heck did you get in?"

"Still got my key, lucky for you," says Nick. "And what the hell is all this?" He spreads both arms in a wide sweep.

Mel sits. Looks at the mess. Empty pizza boxes. Tissues. More beer bottles. "I'm all alone," she says. "Abby's gone. I still don't know where Mum is."

"Well, I'm here now, Slut, we can pick up where we left off. But first we'll get you checked out."

Mel shudders, remembering what a brute he was. Remembering the old days of frequent trips to A & E.

42. Cold Truth

The metal café chairs are cold in the early morning shadows. Jed wears shorts for the first time in weeks. His cast has been removed. He waggles his toes at Brenda. "See, almost ready to trip the light fandango again with you," he says.

She doesn't return his tentative smile. She twists her heavy rings round and around on her plump fingers. She looks down at his once broken leg. Sees the wasted muscles. Sees their wasted time. "Let's take things slowly, Jed," she says. "First we'll get you home. Yes?"

Jed brings the tiny cup of Greek coffee to his lips. He sips the dark bitter brew. "Are you saying our dancing days are over?"

Brenda looks to the distance. Sees the fishing boats returning to the harbour. The gulls clamouring for a share of the catch. One strong bronzed arm raised in recognition.

She swallows hard.

43. He Doesn't Say, She Doesn't Say

Jed wonders what Maria will say when he tells her. She will come at 4 to collect him. He is thankful for all she's done. For showing him island life, introducing him to dolmades and Greek coffee. For teaching him to be a gentle lover.

She enters like a beam of apricot sunlight. Jed sees her cotton sundress dotted with pink rosebuds. Her white sandals on feet the colour of toasted walnuts. Her slim brown ankles. Her scent of jasmine. But he doesn't look at her face. Cannot tell her.

Maria bustles with gathering his possessions. His blue sponge bag. The tartan dressing gown. His black leather slippers. The green striped pyjamas. These are the things she looks at. Not at Jed.

At the hospital door she beckons the taxi. Gently she helps him into the back seat. Then steps back.

With a tinkle of gold bracelets, she waves goodbye.

44. Baking a Cake

Mel is getting ready for her mother's return.

"Please stay," she says to Abby. "Mum will understand."

"You sure?" says Abby, fiddling with the front ties on her yellow pinafore, then slowly stirring her cake mixture, making sure she has the perfect blend of butter and sugar before adding the eggs, flour and milk.

Mel has noticed Abby does this. All the time. Fidgets about with her hands every time they have a serious conversation. She reaches across to her Very BFF Of All Time and gently stops Abby's hands. "Mum will understand," she repeats. "All she ever wants is for me to be happy. And that means having you in my life."

Abby turns, wipes her hands on her pinnie. "What about my happiness though? Has anyone thought of that?"

The only sound in the kitchen is that of the oven pinging away; indicating it is time for the cake to go in.

45. Breaking the News

It is Brenda's last night with Andreas. She has no idea how he will take her news.

"It is time for me to go home," she tries before the mirror. Then pulls a face, gathering her mouth to one side. Sucking her teeth.

She opens a bottle of ice-cold Aphrodite. She takes the tumbler with the wine out to the balcony and looks across to the evening harbour she has grown to love. She wonders if it is the place she loves and not the man. If that is the root of her dilemma.

"Maybe I'll just write him a letter," again she screws up her freckled nose and says to the sky above, "what should I do?"

"About what?" says Andreas, breezing in with a gust of salt air.

Brenda looks him straight in the eye. "I think I must go," she says, and to soften the blow, "my daughter needs me."

46. Hidden in the Fold

Maria presses Jed's white shirts; complex dancing dress shirts with frills down the fronts.

She hears him in her head: "I'm sorry, συγγνώμη, Maria, darling."

Maria bangs the iron down on the shirt, like she's battering Jed's chest. As the tears fall, she releases her grip on the iron. "Why am I doing this? Why am I laundering his clothes for his packing? For leaving with that yellow-haired woman. Am I really such a fool?" she asks herself.

She pours herself a tumbler of Metaxa brandy. As she downs it in one, she smells a tell-tale smell. "Dear God, will he ever forgive me?" she says, lifting the iron from the smouldering shirt.

Right across the front is a large scorch. Maria has left her mark. She feels she has branded Jed as hers. Forever.

She folds the shirt, as she learned in the convent when she was young. Folds, for Jed to discover later, what she has done. And hopefully understand. Much later.

47. Return Journey

They sit together on the flight. She knows he can't, after all he has not long recovered from his stay in hospital, so she lifts his heavy carry-on bag up to the overhead bin, "Jeez Jed, what the hell have you got in here," she says.

"Shshsh… Brend, it's an onyx fireplace."

Brenda nearly chokes on her mint, "A fucking fireplace, Jed, you are fucking kidding me." She sits with a huge hallumph.

He squeezes her hand. She pulls away. "It's in pieces," he says, "we'll put it together when we get home."

"We?" says Brenda, "Jed, there is no WE."

"Don't chew at me, Brend," he says, "I thought we were friends, partners, dancing fandangos."

Brenda says nothing. She cannot imagine them building a fireplace together. She cannot contemplate picking up where they left off. Not after they'd each had their island fling. She thinks of Andreas now with his bronzed muscles and his ready smile. And knows that things will never be the same again.

48. Homecoming

Brenda is in the coffee bar with her daughter.

"You realize you've been gone for the best part of three months, Mum, leaving me all alone to deal with…"

"What? To deal with what? That rotten sod Nick? You've dealt with him, right? Without me, right? I'd say I've done you a good turn, wouldn't you?"

"Mum there's more…"

Brenda looks into her daughter's intense blue eyes, wants to stroke the newly tinted deep auburn hair, wants to gather her up and never let her go. Instead she says, "I think the break did us both good."

"So, you really broke up with Jed?" says Mel.

"And you with Nick?"

"And I found Abby."

"I'm glad," says Brenda. "I too found love. Like you, in the most unlikely place."

She tells her daughter about Andreas, her Greek fisherman. That she will return to him. Very soon. That Mel and Abby should come too.

49. The Letter

Maria bursts into tears. Not for the first time today. Her Jed left her. Last month. The Englishman of her dreams. Flown away with the yellow-haired Brenda. Back to the life he said was far too grey. Away from the sparkling blues and whites of this, her island of love. Her home that she took for granted. Until Jed pointed out, "This is paradise, Girlie, no-one would ever want to leave this."

"Why?" she asks herself. "Why has he gone with that woman? Why did he not stay here with me in paradise? Is it me?"

The letter waits for her on her kitchen table. Placed there with some reservation by her wrinkled, wise grandmother who never approved of the paunchy Englishman who drank much beer.

But she loved her granddaughter and for that reason she hoped the letter would provide all the answers.

50. on waking

a haze of nothing
white no grey
or somewhere in between

where is the pine tree through my window?

a stream of thoughts
of fears

did I 'pass' in the night?
am I on the way to the big hereafter?

this is winter
a time of limbo
a time of still
a time of thinking
of imagining
of wishing
of hoping

a time to admire the extreme
beauty of cold

51. Escape Planning

1st: "Can we fly?"

2nd: "I think it is the only way."

3rd: "But I hate flying."

1st: "I think we could also go by boat."

2nd: "We shouldn't delay, though, I reckon we should scoot. Swiftly."

3rd: "You two fly, I'll take the boat."

2nd: "But what about all for one and one for all?"

1st: "At times like this, we have to be practical. They'll be looking for three old ladies. Not two. Or one alone."

2nd: "I will fly, she can take a bus, and you will take the boat."

3rd: "And when the dust has settled, when they have called off their hunt, we can meet in the city, can't we?"

1st: "Indeed, we will maintain a telephone silence. I will post a message in the personal column at the end of the year."

52. Tea for Three Tra-La

The arrivals for the clandestine 4 pm meeting are sporadic. Dorothy sits very primly alone for twenty minutes, sipping on her cup of Earl Grey. Eventually, Josie weaves her way between tables of steaming teapots and layered cakes and crumby mouths to seek her out. Finally, Gladys, who'd waited too long at the Necropolis, awoke to the fact she was in the wrong meeting place. She bustles through the crowded tearoom not one bit bothered about who might spot her and lands, red-faced, on the third chair at the table.

Without a word they indicate they are happy to see each other.

"Right," says Dorothy, "down to business. You be mother, Glad, while I draw the plan. Josie, you can choose the cakes."

Later, Gladys remembered they'd left the napkins with the plans on the table at The Willow Tearooms.

53. No Hiding Place (In Plain Sight)

The climb up Ben Nevis is not an option. The funicular has to be the answer. "We'll go in separate cars," says Dorothy. "That way they won't see us three old ladies together, and it may confuse the idiots."

At the top Gladys demands a whisky. "No ice," she says to the nice wee girl behind the bar, "I'm cold enough, ta very much."

Josie goes in search of tea-tree oil for her chapped top lip. "Comes from too much kissing," she's told by Dorothy.

"You're only jealous," is her reply.

54. The Big Divide

"You really give me the pip sometimes," says Josie.

"What have I done now?" says Dorothy.

"Well, these wild ideas of yours, that you'll go that way, and she'll go that, and I—well where am I supposed to go?"

"It is time, I think," says Dorothy, "for us each to go our own way. A way for us each to choose. Without my guidance. A time for you to reinvent yourselves."

"Right then, the world is our oyster, is that it?"

"Maybe," says Dorothy. "But really, it is yours and yours alone. I don't think you need me anymore. Think of it as a major turning point in your lives."

Gladys was listening from the guard rail, saying nothing. But as Dorothy disappeared into the mist at Ben Nevis's peak, a hot tear rolled down her cheek.

55. Writer's Block

The author is stumped. Never has she experienced writer's block. She looks through the draft of her novella and sighs. 'This is not the way I wanted it to go,' she says, 'I wanted a happy ending for the three old jail birds, not for Dorothy to disappear into the Ben Nevis mist. Not for Gladys to cry. And certainly not for Josie to show that hidden temper of hers. Not yet, anyway.'

It had started so well for the three perfectly flawed characters escaping from jail, buying the Hebridean tearoom, making a new life for themselves. If she hadn't written in another character—that sneaky reporter from Glasgow—the three old ladies would still be happily baking, serving teas, walking the island shores, not worried about losing their freedom.

'There's nothing for it,' the writer says, 'I'll just have to kill someone off.'

56. Love on a Wednesday

Trish sucks hard on the Scotch mint. She needs to eradicate all hint of Sam. So Johnny won't know.

Every Wednesday Trish goes for her trombone lesson. "Off for my lesson now, Sweetie, see you later," she blows Johnny a kiss.

In reality, Wednesday afternoons are spent upstairs at Ye Olde Bull's Head, on a four-poster bed with bouncy springs. And Sam. She goes home, with a bounce in her step, flushed and satisfied, with a few more bars of Alexander's Ragtime Band under her belt.

Trish is grateful to Johnny. She knows he wanted her to have a hobby; he bought her the trombone and the lessons for her 65th. And they've turned her into another woman.

She bustles around the kitchen making him lamb chops with mashed potatoes, peas and mint sauce, carefully stirring her speciality gravy.

A labour of love.

57. Ginger Biscuits, Navel Oranges, and Chamomile Tea

I am minutiae. A minuscule fragment of a cell. We gather religiously on Monday nights. Enwrapped by our membrane mothers.

Gloria brings ginger biscuits. Tabitha brings navel oranges. I bring loose chamomile tea. We do not leave until the first sliver of dawn breaks the skies.

We fuse like no other clusters within a cell can fuse; our bodies melding, our minds amalgamating. Until we are one being. A united organism: prepared and fuelled to meet the world and correct it.

The night Gloria forgot the biscuits was the initial cause of the breakdown. We began to crumble. The orange peels cracked and juices trickled away down the embankment. The chamomile tea alone provided insufficient nourishment for us to go out and mend the world.

Our membrane mothers said, you are on your own now. Go find your own biscuit barrels and orange groves. Make tea for all.

Be content.

58. Bettina's Perfect Job

She loves her job; not many would, but for Bettina it is perfect.

She is not a people person and hates idle chatter. When she worked in the beauty salon, her days were filled with, 'Going out tonight?' and such questions to which she really was not interested in giving answers.

Bettina gently works the blue shadow around each eye socket, then a touch of blusher, and tint of lip stain. She strokes Mrs. Gretchen Hawkes' face; it looks much less tired than when the lady's remains were first delivered to the funeral home.

'There you are, my dear,' she whispers, 'all ready for the next leg of your journey, you look like a princess.'

Bettina never attends visitations. Never sees the surprise on the faces of the families. Doesn't hear remarks such as, 'She was a beautiful lady.'

But she's pretty sure it is not idle chatter.

59. Scarlet Silk

You've never been on a blind date. You've no expectations.

You choose the scarlet silk dress. You pop it over your shoulders; it slinks its way over your body like a whisper.

Your date waits at the bar; a beer before him. One, maybe two sips gone. He's hunched, as if wary of who you might be, worried, maybe, about the evening to come.

It's good that he's nervous, you tell yourself, but you take a stool on the far side of the bar. You watch. Sip your Muscadet. Slowly. Feeling its freshness. You dab your lips with your handkerchief. He picks at a scab on his cheek.

You make your move.

You shed your scarlet silk with a deftness it deserves, and step slowly into your warm bubble bath. Leaving the bar immediately and coming home was a wise decision, you tell yourself.

But you still wonder.

60. Reggie's Stoop

After supper Reggie takes his bottle of Navy rum out to the stoop. Every night. He sits two steps up, watching the street. Watching the folks go by.

'Hey, Reggie,' Pearlie calls with a wave.

'Hey, Pearlie,' he replies with a wave of his rum-free hand.

Reggie is a fixture in the 'hood. Has been ever since he was just a little whippersnapper. Playing catch with the other kids, Pearlie and Popeye, Frisco and Bennie. With the girls, too.

Later, when they were older, they'd all sit on the stoop talking music, chewing the fat, chewing gum to the beat.

They've mostly gone now. No-one left, apart from Pearlie, to sit on the stoop with eighty-six-year-old Reggie after supper.

He sips his rum, swipes the solitary tear from his cheek, and pats the step on the stoop beside him. Where his friends once sat.

61. The Gown

You finger the delicate fabric. "How much?"

"$65 a yard, Madame."

You sigh. It is truly wondrous; fine with a magical sheen, the colour of buttered sunshine. "I need ten yards," you say, with a hint of a question hidden in your response, hoping for a discount.

The bolt of fabric is carried at an angle, like a jousting stick, to the cutting room.

You watch, holding your breath, as the sharp silver shears slice through the gossamer like rain through cobwebs. It is folded with great care and offered to you wrapped in tissue, tied with raffia.

Weeks pass as your vaporous creation takes shape, stitch by stitch in your loving hands, stopping work as daylight fades into night. Hanging the unfinished gown in the window until dawn.

It is done now. You wait by the door for her to arrive. For her to marvel too.

62. Mary in the Watercress Meadow

Mary Kirk pulls on her gum boots and heads to the watercress meadow. Her sixth birthday is next week; she wants to be a good girl for Mammy and Daddy in the hopes of a party and to invite Clive, Marjorie, Walter, and Jennifer. And Nigel, who might be her boyfriend one day.

The watercress meadow is Mary's favourite place. She listens to the song of the red-throated pipit. Mary knows her bird songs; her grandfather teaches her on their walks. The pipit sings peeze-chwit, peeze-chwit.

Mary doesn't look up, but gathers as much watercress as she can, squeezing the stalks in her fingers, burying her nose in the rich greens, smelling its pepperiness.

"Look, Mammy," she offers her mother the watercress.

Her mother takes the watercress, smiles and says, "Would you like red or yellow jelly for your party? And pink icing on your cake?"

63. Purple Balloons

Purple balloons. Her final wish. A hundred of them tied with silver ribbons to her casket. One for every year of her life. For them to carry her off like dragonflies over the still waters. And for them to burst with joy. One by one.

She'd never had a balloon. And purple was forbidden. She conformed as she was raised. Never a rebel. Never spoke out. Never stamped her foot.

But she swallowed hard many times. Afraid to smile. Frightened to speak. Wanting to sing but not knowing how. Wishing she could dance, but not in the hobnail boots she was forced to wear.

She is in her casket now. Dressed in fuchsia tulle. With golden tassels in her hair, pale silk slippers upon her feet.

If she could, she would sing along to Led Zeppelin playing Stairway to Heaven. And if she could, she would most certainly dance.

64. The Growing Season

Pammie and Daddy prepare the garden. It's spring and their seeds arrived yesterday.

Through the winter evenings they studied the seed catalogues. "Those," she said, pointing to the purple flowers. It is the thing they do together ever since Mummy left.

Daddy rakes the fresh earth. With her little yellow wheelbarrow, Pammie takes away the big stones. She knows that little seeds can't grow through stones.

Daddy makes a single drill along the back of the seed bed, beside the brick wall. "There," he says, "all yours."

Pammie sprinkles her seeds. She piles the rich earth over them, gently patting it in place.

"Grow," she says, watering them from her red watering can.

In June, Pammie's echinacea plants are taller than she is, with an abundance of purple coneflowers. The butterflies love them too.

Daddy watches through the window; the garden, his daughter, her flowers, and the butterflies.

65. Hope

Adam lights yet another cigarette.

"Hoped you were giving it up," says Eve. Bravely.

"Stop nagging and finish your apple," says Adam.

She sees him blow smoke rings. Follows their path as they drift into the sky. Changing shapes. Like messages to other beings. Signals maybe.

He pulls again.

She watches the red glow of the cigarette. Almost down to his fingers now. Eve dreads what will come next and bites nervously into the apple. Doing, as always, what she's told. Obeying Adam's every command. She looks down at her bare arms and legs. She traces the burn scars; the pattern Adam has made with his cigarettes over the months. To let her and anyone else know. That she belongs to him.

She looks back up to the sky with hope. Hope that there is someone to see the signal and get the message.

66. Sales Conferences

You've been on these four-day sales conferences before. Remember Peter? And before that, Dave? All that creeping around hotel corridors after the last drink?

And the next morning at breakfast? They didn't even look at you. Did they?

Those days are over. You found that wasn't the way to promotion. Lessons learned at conferences.

But you can still hear The Management's words: "If you have to drop your knickers to make a sale, then go for it."

You never made salesperson of the year.

Tonight your hotel room door won't lock. You hear the creaking floorboards up and down corridors until the early hours. But you're not taking any chances this year, you drag the heavy oak bureau and wedge it under the doorknob.

At breakfast in the morning you will look them all right in the eye and beam your winning smile.

67. Rain on a Flat Tin Roof

Stephanie bites into the wedge of dark rye bread. She examines the marks her teeth make in the thick layer of butter. Surprised at the unevenness of the pattern. Wondering why her teeth were still as crooked as the Kantara mountains, when her mother had spent a fortune over the years on them.

She tries not to think of what happened to her mother; but it's impossible to forget the night the rain beat down hard on the tin roof. The hammering of the heavy rain, a constant reminder, every storm. Just like tonight.

As if it were yesterday, Stephanie remembers her mother going out into the same beating rain, just like this night, to find Tonto, her little dog. How mother and dog were found after the storm, both drowned in the river that still torrented through the valley.

Stephanie bites again into her dark rye bread.

68. Northern Grit

They talk of Northern grit like it was some kind of dirt. Something to be rid of, maybe a small particle of stone or sand like you'd get in your eye at a railway station with Rachmaninoff's Piano Concerto playing. While Trevor Howard hooks it out with the corner of his very large clean white handkerchief.

Or even a number on the back of a sheet of sandpaper. Layers of impervious shales. To rough stuff up.

No, you don't plan on roughing up anything, or toying with a handsome stranger on a railway platform. Do you?

You'll use your Northern grit for what it is: courage and resolve; strength of character; something that will see you through the bad times. Knowing that there is always good there waiting for you.

You'll grit your teeth, clench that problem. Then spit it out, in triumph, to Jeremiah Clarke's Trumpet Voluntary.

69. Geraldine's Real Purpose

Geraldine thought a bagpipe festival would be a good idea; she knew it could shake up the town in the off season if enough people helped. But more importantly it would get Billy off his arse.

"Git yer pipes out of the shed," she said. "Ye'll need to brush up yer jigs 'n' reels, ye'll be playing in the finale."

Billy shook himself and began practicing his pipes (only because Geraldine told him to).

Geraldine listened from the kitchen window. For eight months. She could tell Billy was improving. The neighbours had stopped complaining and in fact often stopped by the fence to listen.

She toiled to bring the festival to town. Pipers came from across the globe. In their kilts and plaids. The town gave her a volunteer award for bumping up the local economy.

And Billy won first prize for his rendition of Mull of Kintyre.

70. Tuesdays

The Davenport's lorry rattles to a stop. It's Tuesday — delivery day — when Beer at Home Means Davenport's.

A crate of milk stout bottles yodels its way to the back doorstep. The Davenport's man hoists his brown corduroy trousers, preparing for his regular rat-a-tat-tat. But Granny already has the door open. With her whiskery smile, she pays him.

Tonight she pours glasses of the dark-as-liquorice milk stout. With her pinky, artfully stopping the creamy head from waterfalling down to her well-worn tablecloth. She caresses the disappearing embroidery threads, "My mama made this," she whispers, "so they said."

Then she gives a big smile and a "Cheer-ee-ho," as we sup the stout and eat our supper of golden smoked haddock and brown bread and butter.

"I'll keep Grandpa's warm — Tuesdays — always late — Union meetings — mind out for bones," she says in one breath from under a frothy moustache.

We've finished supper when she blurts, "Mama died when I was born, you know, the others brought me up."

I reach for her hand. But she pulls out a bag of caramels, and pops one in her mouth. She doesn't offer one, instead goes to the window, looking for Grandpa coming home. I don't remind her that he's been gone over two years.

She sucks the caramel. Her dentures in the only remaining Crown Derby teacup on the kitchen window ledge.

I haven't told her about my family research. About her mother, my great grandmother being committed and recorded as a 'lunatic' after childbirth with, what would now be known as postnatal depression. Living in an institution well into her eighties.

Again, I reach for my Granny's hand. She passes me a caramel.

71. Minuet in G

The audience hushes. Hans and Myrtle begin their duet for ukulele and cello. Myrtle plays Jacqueline's precious Strad. It overpowers Hans' Gibson. Hans scowls under his handlebar moustache. Myrtle carries on playing, smiling sweetly at the front row. Casting her eyes along the dignitaries. She stops. Staccato.

There is Daniel Barenboim, wearing an ermine trimmed cape, one raised eyebrow, pulling at his earlobe. Myrtle knows the sign.

Myrtle turns to Hans, gives him the nod. With a flourish she indicates to the audience that there will be a ukulele solo, she sets down her instrument, and slips from the stage.

Hans begins Beethoven's Minuet in G.

Myrtle slinks up to Daniel who has also slipped — from the front row. He is behind a potted palm sipping Bacardi and Coke. "There you are," she says.

"Yes," says Daniel, "here I am."

72. Screened In

He makes a tall folding screen with many emerald green stained-glass panels; something for my partial concealment. To see and not be seen, as if standing, or crouching—yes—crouching, or even supine, like in a Delacroix painting, in a forest, behind large-leafed, abundantly entwined undergrowth. Secreted. Pale flesh against the dark. But without the parrot.

"It needs a piano hinge. Here, here, and here," he says. "It will make it more stable."

I look at him then and understand. I understand why he does these things for me. To me. Why he needs me hidden, but not feeling hidden. Why I am his secret. Why he is mine.

And why brass piano hinges will give us stability.

73. The Sparing of the Rod

The order was to carry the large flagon, brimming with sugar-laced tea, to the refectory table. For a twelve-year-old it was a tall order. Nuns lined the walls shooting their evil eyes to my every step.

"You must not spill a drop, not a spot, not a drip," ordered Sister Benedict. "Or you will go into the cupboard for the day."

The cupboard, oh the cupboard, my sanctuary. Away from barking orders and evil eyes. Away from rods that crashed over knuckles for no real reason other than a wrong note while playing Beethoven.

I hum Für Elise in my head, not daring to make a sound. It is when I hit that same wrong note, the G sharp, that my hand quivers, waiting for the rod to strike.

And the flagon tips, slightly, enough for the tea to spill. And send me to safety.

74. Busted

Flash Frank Stubbs takes one last drag on his Mayfair Superking and flicks the dog end out of the window of his classic MG Roadster. It lands by Mrs. Elsie Henshaw's garden gate. Where dear Elsie is standing right now.

"Well, really," she purses her lips and takes her black notebook from her Barbour pocket and jots down the vehicle's details. Because that's her style; renowned throughout the county for her community policing. Busy-bodying some say.

Flash Frank parks behind Ye Olde Bull's Head. Out of sight. He's meeting 'the-back-room-boys,' in readiness for 'the job' they're pulling off that night.

He saunters through his personal back door, all the time in the world, smiling at the thought of the coming night's haul.

But he hasn't bargained for Elsie Henshaw, and half the county's police force already sitting around the table with the boys.

"Busted," says Elsie.

75. Walter's Quest

You need twelve for a set. Walter looks at the row and sees awkwardness and unevenness in eleven. His eyes jump; he'd rather they flow. Without interruption.

And so it is that he sets out to look for the twelfth. He will search the universe if need be, he tells himself with gritty certainty.

But Walter sees the answer in a diagram in the new catalogue on his mother's kitchen table. Of course, it means a trip to Ikea. He takes a number thirteen bus. How he wishes it were a twelve and then his odyssey would be unnecessary.

The brown sheepskin rugs are on sale in aisle fourteen. If only it were aisle twelve. He shakes his head, taking his mother's large shears from his knapsack.

Walter cuts the sheepskin as per the diagram and drapes the cape around his shoulders. His eyes flow. He has the set.

76. Blood, Sweat, and Tears

The day starts sweet. Calm. Relaxed. Early morning sun filtering through. Coffee, ground to perfection. Aroma, to lure the sluggish of men.

Then she loses it. Catching her arm on a rusting nail. Blood spurting like it shouldn't. Hunting for a non-existent bandage. Swearing like she hasn't in years. Heart going like the clappers. Banging doors for no reason. Until they hang on their hinges like a limp line of washing on a becalmed day.

She feels the sweat run between her breasts, puddling around her knicker elastic. Smells its pungency. Hasn't sweated like that in a dog's age. Why does the room swim? Where is he when she needs him? Why does her coffee smell of sweat?

He's here now. Furrowed with questions. She lets the tears fall. Chokes back her words. He places fresh coffee before her. "It'll be OK, I'm here now," he says.

77. Malcolm in his Yellow Jumper.

Julie swivels on her red leather bar stool. The reflection is true. It is Malcolm. In his yellow jumper, knitted by his Auntie Agnes. Julie knows this; they were once a couple. Auntie Agnes made one for Julie too—in the same canary yellow, with cables twisting up the itchy sleeves. Julie's never worn it.

He's seen her. He's heading her way. Beads of perspiration trickle down her neck. She can't do this. Not again. Not now. She doesn't run. For once she stays her ground.

"Been looking for you," he says.

"You've found me."

"Remember the hill?"

"Last thing I need to remember," she says, sliding off the bar stool, grabbing her handbag, heading for the loo.

"I'll order you another." He turns to the barman, as if conspiring.

Julie's in the loo on her phone. 'Come and get me Dad, can you? He's here again.'

78. If Only

If only it hadn't been hot. If only the automatic window locks worked. If only Felix wasn't stupid. I ask you, what kind of ten-year-old takes off his shirt in the car and waves it out of the window like a football scarf?

If only he'd been brought up differently. If only he knew how to occupy his time. If only he wasn't mine.

As we hit the A50, the shirt slipped through his grubby mitts (only grubby because he'd been scratching his way through the earth in the front flower beds just moments before we set off for the funeral), and there it was. Gone. His new expensive white shirt. Blown away like a dandelion clock. Puff.

If only Dan hadn't gone and died. We wouldn't have been going to the funeral at all. No need for the new shirt. No need for anything.

79. Celtic Air

You follow the flow with your fingers. With your eyes. You find no beginning. No end. Yet it's a knot. How can it be? Why?

Now you cannot touch it. It is like a gentle breeze.

It is symbolic; you reconcile yourself with that thought. Like the four directions of the wind. The air knot begins to bind you. To encircle and protect you.

Panic is furthest from your thoughts. You feel no need to escape, but to allow the binding to embrace you. To hold you like a circle of protection. You feel an inexplicable joy.

You have no need to swallow. To taste. To smell. To see. To hear. Just to know.

That there is safety in this nothing.

That the air will hold you.

80. Cat's Cradle

"Play with me. Someone. Please," says Belinda. She has fuchsia pink string tied in a circle, stretched across both hands, her thumbs sticking up.

No-one knows what she is talking about. What does she mean 'play'? It doesn't look familiar, like a card game or dominoes. Does she want us to somehow skip in miniature?

We all shake our heads as if she's bonkers and begin to leave the residents' lounge. We watch through the door.

Just Sheila remains. In her wheelchair by the window. She looks across at Belinda, smiles and says, "I'll play cat's cradle with you."

Belinda scoots over and the two white-haired ladies begin the process of looping the string between finger and thumb, at one stage using the pinky, over and up. Passing the crisscrossed creation on to each other. As if passing a secret.

Lost in their own worlds of childhood.

81. Johnny's Tune

They call out, 'Play us a tune, Johnny.'

He turns his head, looking, through the condensation on the window, to another world beyond. No-one knows his past. And that's the way he likes it.

They call again. Mavis goes to him, gently touches his shoulder. He looks up at her smiling wrinkles.

'One little tune, Johnny, make us all happy again. Pretty please,' she says in her soft Welsh voice.

He stands then, says nothing, shakes down his crumpled jacket, flexes his arms and fingers and steps over to the piano. He doesn't look at them, but runs his fingers up and down the keys, as if getting to know an old friend.

He looks across to the steamed-up window, as if hoping for an apparition, and begins to play As Time Goes By. He seems lost in the melody.

As is everyone; mesmerised by memories.

82. Best Made Plans

I didn't set out to burn the bacon. I didn't set out to drop the toast either. In fact, I didn't set out to do anything; it is supposed to be my day to languish and be waited on. To let Sophia run around in her little black ballet pumps, her slender tanned long but muscled legs and her short frilly white skirt (if you can call it a skirt) and fetch and carry anything I desire.

That was the plan.

But you know what Rabbie Burns said. You don't? Geez I thought you were smart and knew all about this stuff. Anyway, upshot: Sophia can't come. She phoned, had a fall, something to do with her little purple scooter and a guy in a silver smart car.

I suppose I'd better get down to the hospital to Sophia, after all, the bacon sarnie's ruined anyway.

83. Sho Thing, Lady

She can't believe the dust. Red. No-one told her it would be this red.

"It ain't called Red Castle Island for nothing," says her guide, humping her Gucci suitcases off the boat ramp and onto the dusty donkey cart.

Pricilla, known as Prissy, for more reasons than one, says, "That? I'm expected to travel on that?" She points with scarlet talons at the cart.

"Sho thing, Lady, th'only way to travel up to the castle."

Prissy shades her eyes and follows the winding zig-zagging track to the top. There is the castle. Lofty. Red stone. A blue flag flies from the tallest turret. Her heart skips.

"And he's there? Waiting for me?"

"Sho thing, Lady. Name's Richard. Arrived this morning. He said don't forget the brandy."

"I have it here," she says pulling Nathan, her Saint Bernard close, "help me lift him on the cart."

"Sho thing, Lady."

84. The Girl Who Only Wanted to Help

Hooks hang in the shed at the bottom of the garden. Big iron hooks, butchers' hooks, and hooks from a boat long ago.

"Go and fetch me the fertilizer for the tomatoes," says Grandpa, winking, the surest way to get Lizzy to do anything for him. "We want them to be the biggest, juiciest, best tomatoes in The County Show."

Six-year-old Lizzy loves making Grandpa happy, wants his tomatoes to win. The bright yellow can of fertilizer, with a black skull and crossbones on the side, is in the shed, on the highest shelf, far out of Lizzy's reach.

Lizzy does the one thing she's been told never to do; she stands on a rickety old chair. On the very tip of her toes.

The chair tips. Lizzy's caught by the wrist on the sharpest hook. Annoyed, Grandpa finds her lifeless body half an hour later.

85. Oliver's Gifts

Each evening, returning to her cabin after dancing, or joining in the 'fancy dress' night, or enjoying the banjo-playing entertainer, Liz finds gifts. All tied with scarlet ribbons. Delivered from the gift shop by the steward. A gold fountain pen one evening, a soft cream leather designer handbag, another, and so it went for the entire ten-day voyage.

She knows it is the largesse of beaming Oliver, she tries to thank him, he merely winks. Winks? She smiles and mouths, thank you.

They berth at Southampton. In the purser's office, she finds her bar bill has been settled. Amidst the hustle of disembarkation, Liz loses Oliver. And then she sees him with his cabin trunks, looking diminished amidst the crowded pandemonium.

He joins her. Together they stand, the old man and the young woman, on the dockside, beside the old Queen Mary, to say goodbye.

86. The Stalker

She heard the purr when she was halfway across the field. Then she saw the white saloon. Her heart beat relentlessly. Her breathing rapid, and shallow. She knew the car would be there when she reached the road. She could see the driver clearly, a tanned man, with dark brylcreemed hair, sunglasses glinting in the morning sun.

She sprinted then. The car began to accelerate. She knew it was either going to knock her down or the man would snatch her. Like the others.

The Turkish guard was looking out for Suzie; she brought him cake and exchanged smiles and stories. She called him Staffa, short for Mustaffa.

Mustaffa stepped into the road from his guard hut. Holding high his white gloved hand, he called, "HALT."

Suzie slipped in through the gates. The car did a rapid three-point turn and screeched away in a shower of gravel.

87. Blind Date

"What do you think?" he says.

The entire dinner has been scattered with lame conversation: 'Do you prefer limes to lemons?' 'Tabby cats to tortoiseshells?' 'Boats to planes?' 'Bagpipes to trombones?' 'Bedroom windows closed or open?'

Jane knows now, the blind date was a mistake. She should have shaken her head. Not nodded. And here she is opposite a guy who just can't shut up, who eats with his mouth agape, and who asks weird questions without waiting for answers.

"What do I think?" she says. "About what? About the dinner? About the ambience? About the muzak? About your pink striped shirt?"

"No," he says, as if unaware they'd even had dinner. "Us? Do you rate us? At all?"

"Finally," she says, "a question I can answer." Jane stands, reaches for her handbag and heads for the door.

88. The Daughter of Mrs. Crisp

Gillian's mother likes her surname and uses it frequently:

"Here's your crisp white school shirt," she says.

"It's a fine crisp bright morning," she says to Gillian, waiting in her crisp white shirt at the bus stop with the other kids.

"And here's a nice crisp five-pound note for lunch," she folds it and pops it in Gillian's pocket.

"For tonight, I'll wash that crisp fresh lettuce in permanganate of potash to eradicate germs. There's a rhubarb crisp for pudding," she calls in her clipped crisp tones to Gillian who buries her blushing head in her hoody.

Gillian secretly hopes the rhubarb will burn to a crisp then she won't have to choke it down.

She sits at the back of the bus where Alan has saved her a seat and a packet of cheese and onion.

"Bag o' crisps for ya," he says.

89. The Eyes Have It

You look at me with those cold as steel eyes; I try to curb the icy shudder that I know will soon begin to travel my spine. I feel it in my shoulders, in my fingertips. You are freezing my throat.

But wait. Something else stirs.

How could you do this again? Now? Just when things are sorting themselves out. How could you?

It leaves me with no other option—no—don't speak—you've not earned the right. I will do what I should have done a long time ago.

I look straight at you now, right into your eyes. I know – it is the one thing you forbade me to do. With my hot as scarlet molten lava eyes, I look into your icy orbs and feel the control pass. From you to me.

You begin to smoulder.

And you are gone.

I am free.

90. The Day After

He flounders through the start of the day. Searching the kitchen for the right pot for porridge. Wondering which wooden spoon she would have used. Unable to decide if it is Wednesday or Friday.

He is lost without her. He remembers when a sock went missing after the wash. How they searched together in the most unlikely places. How, after a day of doing nothing else, it was found. Reunited with its partner, the pair folded and tucked inside each other. Gently placed in the drawer with a final pat, as if to say, 'welcome back, you were not really lost at all.'

He begins his search. Doesn't even wait until he's had the stiff lumpy porridge; leaving it on the table to go cold.

His mouth is dry with the anticipation of finding her. Of restoring his life to how it once was.

91. One Stitch at a Time

Falling for Gavin is like being very close to the edge of something, she thinks, but then tries not to think.

She always wished to be in love, like all the others, but for Rose it didn't happen. And then, when Gavin took up with Shirley, that was that.

No nights out finishing up behind the bicycle shed for Rose. She stayed home with her mother and knitted hats for newborn babies at the hospital. Watching black and white movies mostly set in railway stations. Making cups of tea to be dunked with a digestive before bed.

Then Shirley was in hospital, she heard. Won't be coming home, they said.

Rose stops knitting hats and begins a navy-blue pullover for Gavin. With each stitch, she falls a little deeper for the man she will soon be kissing.

She hopes he will feel the same.

92. The Fancy Dress Ball

"You're sixteen," Ma said, "it's time you went out more."

I didn't want to go to the sergeants' mess fancy dress ball done up as a 'little Dutch girl', but, being the good daughter they thought I was, along I went.

With my cheeks well rouged, a winged hat of folded paper, and a bunch of crepe paper tulips, I was declared, 'perfect.'

It was fortunate (for me) that Eric was promoted to sergeant just last week. Once the party was underway, with Ma and Pa (dressed as drunken sailors) already two sheets to the wind, I slipped away.

Eric, predictably dressed as a pirate, waited behind the ablutions block with a beer for me. It didn't take long for me to shed the tulips and the origami hat. Or for Eric to cast aside his eye patch.

Yes, indeed, it was time I went out more.

93. Giving Up

Franz is always up to something dodgy. You couldn't like the guy if your life depended on it. He lures you into his schemes every time though. Again and again. With his hypnotic grin, you never stand a chance.

You need to earn a crust. That's for sure. But not like this; Ma will never forgive you.

Later, in the cave sorting through the haul, you ask, 'Why d'ya do this to folks?'

'It's the thrill, man,' Franz says. "Donnit give ya thrills?'

Thrills? You have your own.

The heavy, bejeweled orb leaves your hand, hitting him full on the temples.

Your body heaves like an erupting volcano. You can hardly believe you've taken control at long last. His meagre, unconscious body is curved around the glowing haul.

You brick up the cave's entrance. 'That's an end to it,' you mutter. It feels like you've given up smoking.

94. Petunia, Peach Pie, and Headless Tulips

Petunia skips down the garden path. Plucking the heads from Grandpappy's tulips as she goes. 'Yellow, red, yellow, red...' she sings.

Grammy had said, 'You go wait for Grandpappy by the gate. You tell him to hurry on in now, as I've a slice of peach pie right out of the oven waiting for him.'

At the gate, Petunia proudly offers up her armfuls of tulip heads. 'Red and yellow, Pappy. Just for you,' she says. Making no mention of pie.

Grandpappy is good and mad; his prize tulips are for the big flower show next week. But he hoists his precious granddaughter onto his shoulders and canters with her around the lawn.

'Faster lil' pony, faster, faster,' squeals Petunia with delight.

Grammy is banging on the window, 'I'll give you pony,' she yells, 'no pie for either of you now.'

95. The Search for Eternal Life

Pamela moans. It's not her idea to ride donkeys up Mount Olympus in search of the spring. The group decided without her at camp last night. "The waters will give us eternal life," they concluded.

But now, after a week of searching through the dense cedar forest, most fall by the wayside and leave her to it.

Wild rosemary edges the twisting, climbing trail to the summit. The donkey stops. It lowers its head, draws back its plump, black top lip exposing long browned gnarled teeth, and chews. Pamela loses her grip of its halter and flings her arms around its rough and sour-stinking neck. There's a sheer 4000-foot drop into the ravine below. She hears the waterfall. The spring cannot be far off. She craves water.

The group find her a week later, just feet from the spring. Grazed and bruised.

The coroner's report: Dehydration.

96. Stop the Bus, You Want to Get Off

You must dig deep to remember. Closing your eyes against white lights, visualising the day it happened, you see it all now in panoramic technicolour.

"She was with me," you say, "Mama, she was on the coach beside me."

The light goes out. Even with your eyes closed you know. Shuffles are all you hear. But you continue, "We were driving through Glencoe. Mama talked to me about the massacre then. For the first time. I had no idea."

You speak no more but let that day in your head continue. You are there, alighting the coach. Gazing across the glen through the mist. Hearing the screams of anguish as clans tear each other apart. Smelling their blood.

Now all you hear are bagpipes playing Flower of Scotland. You don't wipe away the tear that rolls down your cheek, you taste the salt. And remember.

97. Cakes for Convent Girls

They arrived each month in shining cake tins. Victoria sponges, Dundee cakes, lemon and ginger loaves. Other boxes contained eggs and Marmite.

Deliveries from home supplemented our basic rations of Greek bread, tinned butter, and weak tea. As eleven-year-old boarders at a French convent in Nicosia, we had to be made of tough stuff. But food from home was eagerly anticipated.

The cakes always arrived riddled with ants. That's Cyprus for you: ants, scorpions, cockroaches, snakes. They got into everything. We were used to them.

A wall ran around the outside of the refectory, it was wide enough for us girls to sit and dangle our legs, kicking the ancient golden brickwork, scuffing our Clarks sandals, guarding our cakes that the clever nuns had placed in a row on the wall in the beating sun. Watching the ants scarper for dear life.

Waiting for that unforgettable first slice.

98. Edith's Revenge

She joined Hank's band at fifteen, playing the spoons for dances on Saturday nights.

She married that drunkard Karl at seventeen. "You ain't goin' no more," he said, "you're my wife, I ain't havin' no more bullshit."

She told no-one of the way he treated her, never revealed her scars; the imprints from his belt buckle were on parts of her body well hidden from friends and family.

Hank was on the radio, she played along with her spoons, ready for Karl when he burst in yelling "I told you woman…"

Blasting Karl's stubbled face to smithereens with the ready-loaded shotgun as Hank yodelled, *When my Blue Moon Turns to Gold Again*, earned her thirty years.

"But it was worth it," she said, her eyes sparkling along with her spoons.

99. The Seven Sisters

Father passed his driving test and immediately decided to take us on holiday in our new car. It was a secondhand Morris Minor, and we were going to the mountains.

The road from Troodos down to Paphos was called The Seven Sisters; it had seven hairpin bends. Not great for a new driver. But we trusted Father.

Loose stones skittered into the chasms bordering the road every time Father braked. We all sang a lusty, 'She'll be coming down the mountain…' Unaware that with a twist, the steering wheel had come off in Father's hands.

He stopped dead. In the middle of the road.

"You'd all better get out and wait under the trees while I fetch help," he said, striding off in the direction of Paphos waving the steering wheel over his head.

It was sixty-five years ago, as clear as if it were yesterday.

100. When the poet turns 100

It is years since she wrote. She has little memory now but something wriggles, worms. Words? Oh where is Timothy when she needs him?

Sounds trickle down a spiral with ten thousand thoughts like gentle rain. She sees gnarled hands of a sage, moving stones around the table, playing games, telling wise stories.

Fables.

Myths.

In the dimness, dancing petroglyphs circle her head.

Distant voices chant the wrong words.

Does she hear the drums? Do they speak to her?

She taps her foot with the rhythm but feels nothing.

"Happy Birthday to you…" sing the faces around her. Flames illuminate their apple cheeks, their sparkling eyes. "Blow them out. Make a wish," their red mouths say.

She blows as she is bid. She wishes she could wish. She watches the large knife dig deep into the yellow flesh of the cake.

And closes her eyes.

101. Piano Exam Etudes

She tries to play it fast. It is supposed to be the speed of The Andrews Sisters singing about a bugle boy.

She turns off the YouTube link. Disheartened. Disillusioned. Surely this is a bluesy, piece of swing music. Rattling through it like she's in the 400 metres at The Commonwealth Games isn't going to win her prizes if she falls at the first hurdle. Is it?

"It's too late to change your mind," says her piano teacher. Gently. "You've worked too long on this one."

The music book arrives in today's mail. *Alternatives to the Etudes* on the shiny blue cover.

There are three weeks to go before the exam. Her mouth waters as she sees the theme to Love Story is an alternative to her too fast and furious boogie.

She sits at the piano: Where Do I Begin, ripples with ease from her arthritic fingers.

102. More to Life than Money

There is little room in his hectic life for love. Money is the all-important factor. Making money. Counting money. Spending money.

Turning pennies into pounds. Buying low. Selling high. His evenings are a swift balancing act sandwiched between a pie and a pint at his local. Watching but not seeing the smiling beery faces around him. Hearing but not listening to the laughter of ordinary folk out after a day's work.

The flat is stainless steel stark. The air cold and stale. The silence colourless in every way.

Wednesday, on impulse, he leaves the flat and returns to the Dog and Duck. Miranda is perched at the bar in a red off-the-shoulder dress.

She turns. Smiles at him. At that moment he knows he must make room in his life for love.

103. This Land is Your Land

The land is his now. He stands by the boundary marker and looks down over the fields towards the lake. Then up to the stand of tall pines cresting the hill.

Something feels wrong. There was no need for Biff to leave him the land. When he got the call about the will, he nearly dropped off the stoop, the stoop that was rotten and could cause him to fall and break his neck any day.

And a fall would be a blessing to Cyrus. That would be an end to it all, now that he's down to his last dime.

Then it's Biff who drops dead instead. Biff who has everything.

Biff who leaves 128 acres of prime land to Cyrus in his will.

Cyrus stands by the boundary marker and surveys the land, looking for Biff coming over the hill waving his hat.

But Biff doesn't come.

104. Mother's Boy

You make a note of her number; she has a nice smile, white teeth, and tiny diamond stud earrings. Not those great dangly things like chandeliers rattling around the face like most girls these days.

Mother would approve. Not too loud, good deportment with shoulders back. Definitely not a sloucher. But was she too willing to give you her number? Too forward? Mother wouldn't like that.

You put the note in your parka pocket and head home. You'll decide later.

Mother has tea on the table. You slip off your shoes by the back door and wash your hands. You sit opposite each other, backs straight. No elbows on the table. Silence while eating.

Years later, you'll find the note at the bottom of your parka pocket along with the fluff and hairs that belong there.

And you'll wonder.

105. Comfort Food

Louise stirs the pot. Her mind is elsewhere. She wonders where her Graham is.

Regardless, when he does come home she will, at least, have a good warming pot of soup ready. Her eyes leave the window and the gloom of dawn, and she looks down at the simmering liquid.

Hours before, after the talk with the police, she'd chopped and sweated the leeks, onions, celery, garlic, and carrots before adding the cooked chicken and the most important ingredient, the home-made bone stock.

Her hand trembles as she gently stirs. She breathes in the aroma, knowing she has one of her best soups ready for Graham when they do find him.

In the weeks, months, and years to come, Louise will always associate that aroma with her loss.

106. Nothing to Lose

Brian hauls his sports bag and racquets out to his bike. He aches in every muscle. He thinks he may have a fever too. The last thing he wants on this sunny Sunday morning is to take part in a squash tournament. But the bets are on and if he doesn't win this final round, he loses everything.

He pedals, best he can, to the sports-centre. The breeze through his helmetless hair cools him down somewhat. He barely notices that he's shivering.

The squash courts are in sight when the trembling sets in. Brian wobbles on his bike. Wobbles is an understatement. The kerb rushes at him like a freak tornado.

The pathologist's report is straightforward: Advanced stages of Lyme Disease culminating in loss of mind and muscle control resulting in a fatal blow to the head.

107. Wedding Jitters

Glenys stands before the mirror. She rarely looks at herself.

The dress is simple, not white, the salesgirl called it ivory. "This is what you wear when, well, you know…" she said, patting Glenys's barely see-able baby bump.

"And now the veil and train," she said. "How about something elegant?"

Glenys stood tall. The salesgirl affixed the headpiece. She arranged the long train, also ivory. It cascaded down Glenys's back in a gentle flurry of butterflies.

"Yes," said Glenys, who wished her mother was with her to nod approval. "That's perfect."

It's the big day. Grey. Threatening rain. Glenys looks again in the mirror. The dress is getting tight across her bump. She lets the veil fall over her face. Hiding her tears. She wonders if she could, somehow, trip over the train's cascade of butterflies, thereby solving many problems.

108. There's a Story in Everything

The guys are in the cellar putting in a new furnace. Ellen's glad she waited until June, when there'd be no need for heat, but she still paces the floor.

She watches as a young guy with a punk hair-do carries a long pipe out to his van.

Ellen knocks on the window, "Leave that here, don't take it away, my Harold put that in fifty years ago."

The young guy shakes his head, in the way young guys do when they think old folks are batty, "OK, Ma'am," he says.

Just before the sun dips on this longest day, they leave. Ellen inspects the work, nods, and picks up one end of the long copper pipe. She puts on her reading glasses to find and kiss the words Harold had scratched in with his jack-knife all those years before: Harold Loves Ellen 21/6/63.

109. Martha's Blog

Martha can't reach high D. She blames the electric carving knife. It was that Sunday when Roger didn't come home. The joint went cold, the crispy roast potatoes lost their crisp and the gravy congealed.

She didn't blame Roger; how could he know she would soldier on when he was gone with his fancy bit from the Red Lion?

No, it was the lethal carving knife to blame.

Getting back to this high D. It's the highest D on her piano: a problem for Martha who is now a few fingers short of a handful. Thanks to that carving knife.

But Martha is a 'thinks outside boxes' gal. High D? No longer a problem. You can read all about it on her blog: Less is more – piano playing with missing fingers.

110. Pity about the Pudding

You walked with her to the end of Castledine Street Extension and through the playing fields following a path by the brook.

The path was blocked, there was a wheelbarrow in the way. You scooted around it on your thin little legs. But she wasn't nimble at all; four feet tall and almost as wide.

Edging around the wheelbarrow, she lost her balance, screamed, and fell into the brook.

You remember only scant details of the incident. It was seventy years ago after all. An ambulance. A nice policeman who took you home, who switched off the oven, removed the rice pudding with its burnt black skin, opened the windows to let out the smoke. And the smell.

To this day, the smell of burning milk reminds you of that day. And Grandma.

She came home bruised, with her head bandaged. 'Pity about the pudding,' she said.

111. You Were a Chief Gumster

To be a gumster you needed to dissolve a fruit gum in your mouth as slowly as possible. No sucking. No chewing. For an eight-year-old that was a challenge.

The one who lasted the longest was a Chief Gumster.

You've not seen a packet of fruit gums for sixty-five years. How they remind you of the old country, just looking at the wrapper brings back memories of the village, of the murder on the playing fields, of Unchained Melody playing over and over in your head.

You open the end of the roll. Hoping the first fruit gum is green, your favourite. It is. You are immediately taken back to childhood with that first taste.

You've no idea how you made one last that long as a child, for in five minutes you've chewed your way through the lot. But the memories linger on.

112. Zigzag Rickrack

To make a pinafore at school you needed all the right notions. The correct colour thread, tape for the ties and most importantly, rickrack braid for the trim.

Your pinafore is yellow, you choose a contrasting royal blue for the trim. It takes a steady hand to guide it along all the edges as the sewing machine whirs faster and faster. You have no control over the machine's foot pedal; it has a mind of its own.

You will always have the scars. The zigzags up your arms. The memories of the mad needlework teacher slinging you out into the corridor for being a 'stupid girl.'

There were a few inches of the blue rickrack left over that day. They are at the bottom of your sewing box. They've never seen daylight in all these years.

It is time to face that demon.

113. Dependable Beige

Her name summed her up, or so they said. Why her parents named her Beige was beyond the family. "Looked it up in a book," they said. "It means dependable."

She was lumbered with it. Not that it bothered Beige. In fact, she used it as her brand: 'Dependable Beige.'

When clients visited, they were not surprised at the decor, the mushroom paintwork, the oatmeal curtains, the buff carpets.

One Saturday, Beige donned her fawn mac, slipped on her brown shoes, and popped on the bus to the shopping mall.

She said, afterwards, it was like someone had lifted a veil, albeit a cream veil, as when she saw the arrays of satin cushions and home accessories, temptation was too great.

In Beige's office now, displayed with some panache, are sparkling rust-coloured cushions. Sitting in a row on parade.

Her clients ask if she is still dependable.

114. The shape of things that come (and go)

"Can you stop clipping the box hedge like that, Alex?" says Miranda.

"Stop?"

"Yes, my dear, I'm not loving all the sharp lines. Let's think about peacocks and turtle doves."

Alex scratches his head and puts the clippers away in their box in the square shed attached to their little, square house.

Miranda sings about 'little boxes, little boxes….' Alex gets the message. Over the months he adds a front porch with gingerbread trim. He builds a Victorian style conservatory on the back. Soon their little box of a house is swallowed up by curlicues and fanciness.

Outside, the box hedge has become a menagerie of exotica: a giraffe guards the ornate wrought iron gate. Two lions roar side by side. Birds of paradise totter in the gaps and Miranda has to use a walking stick to thrash her way through.

"Maybe next year we should declutter," she says.

115. Alan's Progression

"When one door closes…" Gloria stops in mid cliché.

Alan grimaces. Along with clichés, he gags at misplaced apostrophes. He knows he should never have fought with his editor over just one wee one. There are times, he tells himself, when you just have to give in to progress.

Alan has no publisher for his squeaky-clean manuscript. There are no open doors on his horizon, nor windows either for that matter. I wonder, he tells himself again, if I should throw caution to the wind and sail off to Nauru. He'd never heard of the island until the other night when it was an answer on a gameshow on the telly.

The smallness of the island and the simplicity of the idea give him hope. He walks through his front door into the wide blue yonder.

To hell with the cliché, he tells himself.

116. Stop the world, the cat needs feeding

Please can you feed my cat, I'm going away, says the note on the doormat.

Jeff scratches his head, he doesn't know his neighbours, has never seen a cat. He pours a bowl of Cheerios but has no milk. He eats them dry, asking himself if cats really do drink milk.

He dresses and leaves for town. The bus-stop has a notice: Buses Cancelled. He bikes it. There are notes on all the shop doors: Closed. Sorry.

Jeff pedals home, hoping he still has that old can of sardines.

There is no sign of life in any form for the entire ride.

Until there, on his doorstep, he sees a flutter of white paper. A note. Holding it down is a black cat with yellow eyes. The cat is bigger than a beer barrel.

The note reads: Feed me. Now.

117. It's all about dead bodies today

Betty sits on the riverbank contemplating her parents' discussion around the table last night. She kicks at the skeleton. She knows it was a porcupine from the shower of quills along the gravel edge. She toes the curved spine, perfect in its formation and wonders what kind of brain was once in that small skull.

Alongside the spread of bones is an unmoving chickadee. 'Must've been hit by a car,' the ten-year-old murmurs, reaching down to stroke its minute head of still silky but dead feathers. She touches its beak, smaller than a grain of corn.

Betty remembers last night's heated talk then. About the poor crop. How there'll be no money for anything. How Ma said she'll go back East and take Betty with her.

How Pa said, "Over my dead body."

118. He'd have liked that

As Billy reaches for his drink, ash drops from his cigarette on to Frannie's black silk skirt. Frannie doesn't notice. She's coming to terms with the bombshell.

"I'll take you to the grave if you like," he says.

"My son has a grave? Should I take flowers?"

"He'd like that," says Billy.

"Give me one of those," she says. "Please."

Frannie pulls hard on the cigarette. Breathes deeply and closes her eyes. "I should have come here sooner," she says, dropping her ash, too, on her black silk skirt.

"He'd have liked that," says Billy.

"What else can I take?" she says.

"A beer," says Billy. "He always liked a beer."

They stand over the fresh earth of her son's grave. "I should have loved you more," she says.

"He'd have liked that," says Billy.

119. Body Language

"I can find you a place far away from prying eyes," says Bonnie.

Gemma nods. They travel all day and reach the island as the sun sets.

"Will it do?" says Bonnie.

Gemma nods and pours the whisky. "Will you stay?" she says.

Bonnie nods and sips her drink. "It will make a fine bolt hole for you. That is what you wanted, isn't it?"

Gemma nods, "It's that obvious?"

"You don't have to say another word," says Bonnie.

They sit in the half dark, sipping their drinks, not speaking. The view of the mainland just a black smudge on the skyline.

120. They Told Themselves

'Lash extensions are the answer to all my problems,' Carl tells himself.

The house sleeps. He slips fifty dollars from Paula's purse. Stuffs them into his pocket. 'Should be enough,' he tells himself.

It's too early for the bus. Hitching a ride it has to be. He stands on the corner. Thumb up. 'If only I had eyelashes to flutter now,' Carl tells himself, 'they're really gonna change my life,' as trucks and SUVs thunder by.

It's a pearlescent SUV that gets him. Driven by Sophia on the school run, replenishing her mascara. 'If only I'd looked,' she told herself.

121. The Forest Green Door

When life's good, time flashes by. But now, when life couldn't get much worse, things stand still: sorrow in an ice cube.

You stand on the overgrown garden path looking at your back door, as if in a trance, watching the first flake of forest green paint flick at a corner, curl and fall in slow motion.

Years ago, you bought the paint in great quantities in a sale. You were both young, excited, vibrant, and full of plans. Every three years, sanding down and repainting, 'keeping it fresh,' you said. 'Cared for.'

Since she's been gone, the caring went too. 'Let the paint flake and fall,' you say. 'What was it all for anyway?'

Then you remember: all the good times, racing through life at a breakneck speed. Eating it up. Sunshine. Laughing. Painting the backdoor forest green.

Loving.

122. Neil's Way

Neil plays Sudoku every morning before breakfast. He never makes an error. He is swift but very particular about how he makes each pencil mark.

To be ready, he sharpens his HB pencil with a scalpel the night before. Each shave of the wood is exact. As he pares, he counts each pale peel and adds it to the blue glass jar on the window ledge. Like trapped creatures deprived of oxygen.

Neil keeps his completed Sudokus organised in an old cabinet with many shelves. It was used in the 1930s in a post office to store stamps and receipts. To begin with, he was concerned that the old musty smell might pollute his pages.

But now he feels it makes them more perfect. It has given them an aroma. A life. He has brought them alive.

Neil wonders where this will all lead.

123. Regina's Legacy

Regina was a spinster, or so people thought. Her garden gate swung on squeaky hinges twice a week when she went shopping. That's all.

She was a keen gardener and grew exotic plants from exotic seeds that she procured from who knows where. And they grew and grew until her garden was like a rain forest.

After her death machetes were used to hack a way through. The neighbour hackers were shocked to find another dwelling deep in the undergrowth. A young gentleman sat at the doorway whittling cricket bats and stacking them sideways beside what could only be a wax effigy of a nude Regina Wilson.

When asked, he introduced himself as Will Wilson, then, seeing their perplexity, explained the effigy was made by the two of them, years before, for this occasion.

The neighbours could see she was undoubtedly ugly. And that, as they say, explained everything.

124. Chrissie's Happiness

To unlock the door to happiness you need a key. Not just any key. But a unique artefact. Handmade by Justin and left for you in a special place.

Chrissie tells this to Alexa. She hopes Alexa will understand because Chrissie doesn't have a clue what it means. Chrissie thinks this is all really a load of bunkum.

"Alexa, isn't it a load of bunkum?" she says as precisely as she can to her new kitchen gadget.

"I'm sorry," says Alexa. "Bunkum is not available on tune-in." And without any warning bursts into a Louis Armstrong number.

Chrissie shows her delight by swaying around the kitchen in a soft shoe shuffle. In fact, she is over-the-moon happy. So happy she is not one bit bothered about Justin, artefacts, special places. Or the key to happiness at all.

125. Tunnel Vision

Valerie pushes her hair out of her eyes. She wishes she had ribbons, wishes for many things like shoes to help her walk across the hot rocky ground.

She has no idea how she got here. Or when. All she knows is the poly-tunnel has no beginning. No end.

Hoops support the opaque covering. Valerie stops her tortured walk, looks closer at where the hoop enters the scorched ground.

"Yes," she says through parched mouth and blistered lips. "I don't need to find the end; the answer is right here."

She begins to dig.

126. The truth was in the cherry stones

"I can't tell the kids," says Jess, "they really want to go on this trip."

"Nothing we can do," says Tony. "No money means no money."

"But they've worked very hard, fundraising. Where has it gone?"

"Search me," says Tony.

Jess thought about his nonchalance. About his new Apple watch. She didn't dare think further.

Jess didn't tell the kids the trip was off. She pawned the rings Tony had bought her over the years. She didn't know they'd be that valuable.

She wishes she'd taken more heed of the cherry stones before marrying a thief.

127. Mother's Day

"I've told you before, do not lean against the car, you'll scratch it," she screams.

Max rolls his eyes. His mother screams at him all the time now. He hates it when she does; her face goes beetroot and her turkey neck wobbles.

He sighs and heaves himself from the gleaming royal blue coachwork of his mother's limousine. Well, not his mother's exactly, it just comes with her job. How he wishes things could go back to normal, before she became this high-powered government official with a flag on the bonnet and a guard in the front seat.

It was lucky to have the car to themselves for the day. He'd hoped they'd go to McDonald's. After all it is Mother's Day.

"Can't risk it," she'd said.

He leaves the bunch of daffodils on the front seat and walks into town alone.

128. If…

If only they'd each been content with their lot
If only he hadn't told her in the first place
If only she hadn't bothered to listen
If only he hadn't bought her a drink
If only she'd said, 'No thanks'
If only he hadn't made the suggestion
If only she hadn't offered to switch
If only the weather had been fine
If only she'd had her brakes checked
If only he hadn't been on the phone
If only it was Thursday not Wednesday
If only he'd had a good night's sleep

*

If only there wasn't that nip in the air
If only she'd stayed home
If only she hadn't walked to the edge
If only she'd listened to Mike

*

What if he'd insisted?
What if he'd held Sophie close?
What if he'd whispered?
'What if something happens to you?'

129. A Little Dab

He wore Brylcreem when I first met him, with his thick head of deep mahogany tresses, he really didn't need it. But, "A little dab'll do ya," he sang, out of tune, at the bathroom mirror. "You'll look so debonair. The girls will all pursue ya…"

From my point of view it was disgusting. OK, he styled his hair 'til he looked like Elvis. But still, it felt greasy, even more so when it flopped into your face at strategic moments. I certainly didn't want to 'get MY fingers in his hair.

Then Cossack arrived on the scene. Everything changed. The bathroom choked with the pongy hairspray morning and evening. Preening and puffing himself like Liberace.

The girls certainly didn't pursue him then either.

130. Deceptive Appearances

Well, I did say the girls didn't pursue him, didn't I?

The Elvis look-alike became a hermit for a while. Living in a hut (made out of flattened cooking oil bottles) in the middle of a sparse wood of birch saplings—so he could be seen from miles around. He thought not.

He began braiding his hair then, Rastafarian style, working it with his gnarled fingers while seeing his reflection in the bottom of a biscuit tin.

I knew this because I'd been watching him. Through the trees. With my binoculars.

I guess he saw the glint because before I knew it he was inviting me for tea.

"I'm Giles," he said in a university accent, pouring me an Earl Grey into a bone china cup with pansies around the rim.

And I wondered then if I'd judged a bit prematurely.

131. Grandfathers Know Best

"A June wedding is not a good idea," says her gardener grandfather. He doesn't explain. It has been his method of teaching since Angela was a toddler. That's how she learned to say mesembryanthemum at four years old.

Angela does not change the date. She's nailed Rodney down to June 6th despite his snide comment about D-Day. "At least you'll remember it," she says.

The florist scratches his head. "Lupins are the best I can do," he says. "I may just find a gardenia bloom for your hair."

The bridal march is belting out at full throttle as her father marches her down the aisle where Rodney (phew that's a relief) is hopping before the altar rail.

But all Angela sees are the sad drooping lupins. Their tips bowed over touching the stone flagstones of the church floor.

And she understands what her grandfather meant.

132. Veneer

It was a 'marriage made in Heaven.' But Margo, keeping her own counsel, saw beneath the veneer of the fancy multi-bedroomed (with large family plans) mansion, the oriental carpets, the slick new his'n'her cars parked in the double garage. And, naturally, under the stainless steel and granite of the super-designed, but unused, kitchen.

She's been allowed to visit her daughter just once. But now Priscilla's phone call, 'I'm tearing my hair out Mummy,' brings her running. Well, more gurgling up in her sunshine yellow vintage VW Beetle.

That's when she finds Priscilla, with exactly that, her hair pulled out, all over the Italian marble floor, missing a Persian rug by a whisper.

"What?"

"He's a pig Mummy."

"You're coming home with me."

"But what about…?" Priscilla waves her trembling hand around the expensive dwelling.

"It's only a veneer," says her mother, finally speaking her mind.

133. Triangulation

In the rush to grab an instrument for orchestra, Bridget was pushed aside. All that was left for her was a triangle.

"It is in D Major," said the kind music teacher.

She held it by the ribbon loop and struck it with its beater. She found it wasn't a simple thing to play but over time became so accomplished she was asked to play the solo in Hannikel's Triangle Concerto.

On Sunday she stands on stage, before the cellos and double basses. She wears a little black dress. Her streaming red hair gleams in the stage lights. Her triangle glints in the spotlight.

The performance is second to none; everyone says, standing for the ovation. It is just a shame that Bridget's long red hair catches and tangles in the cellist's bow as they leave the stage.

134. Bowl Cut

It wasn't a death wish, more a desire. Aaron wanted to be like the other kids. To be more boy-like. He sat at the kitchen table watching his mum beat a pancake batter.

"Would you like orange boats?" She said, not looking up from the creamy contents in her mixing bowl.

Aaron wasn't thinking about orange boats. Nor watching his mother pour the batter into the sizzling buttered pan. Not seeing the pile of golden pancakes on the serving platter. Not salivating as normal. He was eyeing the perfect bowl.

That afternoon he took it and his mother's pinking shears to the bathroom. He pulled the bowl centrally over his long blond curls. The exposed curls he chopped off with the shears.

Exhilarated, he shook his head like a happy pony.

His mother did a fair amount of head shaking too.

135. The Old Man at Number 44

Lily always thought of him as 'such a nice old man,' weeding his front garden mornings when she went to catch the school bus. Smiling at her. Waving sometimes.

She began waving back in the summer just before school broke up. That's when he came to the garden gate and she saw his eyes of flint grey, hard as rocks despite his smiles and waves.

Lily was polite, "Mum's expecting me at 4.15," she told him when he invited her in for ginger cake. "Just the colour of your beautiful hair," he'd said, rippling his fingers through the air.

During the holidays she didn't walk his way. A summer job kept her busy. In September she saw his house all boarded up. A 'for sale' sign stuck in the overgrown flowerbeds.

When asked, no-one knew where the nice old man in number 44 had gone.

136. Close Quarters

When Claudia read about the photographic exhibition themed 'Close Quarters,' she invested in a close-up filter.

For weeks she scoured the neighbourhood for inspiration. She crawled around in the dirt taking photos of beetles, dandelion seed heads, and cracks in pavements.

But she felt nothing really hit the mark.

She sat on the balcony of her high-rise looking across at other high rises and wished the theme was 'Distant Views.'

Then it hit her.

She removed the close-up filter and replaced it with her most powerful zoom.

And there she was. Through the windows and in the bedrooms of other high-rise dwellers. Capturing action shots at such close quarters it could make the hair stand up on the back of your neck.

She called her grainy black and white collection, 'Close Quarters from a Distance.' The exhibition organisers were delighted at her unique approach.

137. The Real Thing

Lionel hums Love me Tender. He's been humming the same old first line for the past hour. Louise throws a cushion at him.

"Sorry," he says, "thought you didn't like this programme."

"I don't, I think it's absolute trash, but honestly Li, so is your humming."

She turns off the TV. Lionel stops humming.

"Will you cut my hair then?"

Louise grins, "Thought you'd never ask."

Lionel sits on a kitchen chair on the balcony with a tea towel around his bare shoulders. He looks across the city seeing flickering lights through windows. "Everyone must be watching it," he says.

"Good," says Louise, appearing on the balcony with her hair clippers. She is completely naked. "Means they won't be watching us then."

She clips Lionel's hair, letting the long fair locks float away like dragonflies on the breeze.

"This is better than a trashy movie," he says.

138. A Week Away

They call the boat Hebe (as in heebeegeebee). She's actually called Florence III according to her peeling paint.

She's a canal boat. The gals have rented her for a week away. And they really need to get away. They've loaded her with a case of wine and a bumper bag of chocolates along with other essentials and are determined to forget everything. Except each other.

Hebe's tied up at the Coventry basin mooring by 11 pm. No-one else is there. The moon shines down in all its glory on the flat black waters of the canal.

Josie has brought along a bottle of bleach. "Time to really wash those guys out of our hair," she says.

And they do. Every hair on their bodies is bleached by dawn.

"We need never go back," says Sandy.

"Did you ever intend to?" say the others in unison.

139. Dragons

He advertised in the paper, I hired him to split wood. I expected a brawny lumberjack in a red plaid shirt. And a beard. Maybe. With an axe.

Three cord of wood takes a fair bit of splitting in my book, when he told me it'd take just a couple of hours, I suspected then he wasn't the real deal.

I'm not sure what powered the beast. It was green with cogs. The noises it breathed with its billows of steam reminded me of the old days at the station when the Edinburgh train snorted in. And out. Like a dragon.

When the wood was all stacked, I said, "Coffee?"

"I prefer tea," he said. He held his cup (no mug thank you) delicately, thanked me for my cheque, left his card and drove away in his Alpha.

There's a shiny axe by the woodpile.

140. You are that man in a bar

You sit with melancholy. Looking into the abyss, while Missy in the bright white shirt looks on.

She pours wine. You do not see the glass, the lass, you seek the past.

There is no future in full-bodied Bull's Blood wine but a hankering for goulash wafts then drifts on by with other tastes of memory.

You'll remember days when you sat around a checkered table sipping bread-scooping rich herb-scented gravy.

Stand, tip the white-shirt girl. Smile. Offer thanks for succour taking you through the gloom and out into the place you need to be.

141. Climax

Rachmaninoff surges through Brief Encounter. Arpeggios climax. You hold your breath smelling cold railway station coffee in that finite moment.

Your connection between music and life where social networking, texting, and unreal reality TV hold no finite moments for you.

Then you find, seated upstairs on a red London bus, there is a higher level from which you may view the world; watching life through soft-lighted windows without curtains. In each embrace, each scowl, each tear, each laugh you will hear Rachmaninoff's Piano Concerto rise beyond the first climax.

And a thousand voices rise in harmony singing Zadok the Priest.

142. Für Elise

The nun lies on her deathbed. It won't be long before she meets St. Peter who will acknowledge how well she's educated the young, how thwacks with canes deterred wrong notes.

She hears Beethoven's Für Elise. She drifts back to her days of teaching piano. To naughty girls without feeling for music. Her fists clench. She slaps the sheets, like she flapped her habit, stinging the girls' faces.

It is not time, her Lord is not ready. Not until she feels the wrath of the women who will arrive with canes to administer their judgment on her aged, helpless hands.

143. An Impossible Choice

"This is what's available," barks the man.

She looks through the bars.

Pressed against them: faces. Beseeching. The heart-breaking whining unbearable. She cannot take them all.

She writes a random number on her document. Presents it to the office.

"A boy? You pick a boy?"

"Yes," is her choked reply.

144. Swiftie

Arthur is a black greyhound. He lives with Polly, his woman. She watches videos of his previous life; racing in Florida.

"There gooooes Swiftie," screams The Starter.

Arthur flies, his muscles rippling. He chases Swiftie, the lure.

Arthur never catches Swiftie, never wins—he's retired at two years old. A failure.

Polly is at Walmart. She spots the squeaky fluffy bunny in the pet toys.

"Here's your very own Swiftie," she tells Arthur.

Arthur rips and tears the stuffed brown bunny like a hound incensed, finishing with a big swallow of the squeak.

Written all over his face: success.

145. Blackie, the Underneath Rabbit

Blackie liked being under something. Usually under the grand piano. Except when it was time for Norman's piano practice after tea. That suited Blackie just fine. Then he hopped, as bunnies do, into the kitchen where Norman's mammy sorted out unwanted leaves from the day's veggies. She gave them to Blackie under the kitchen table.

But today, after tea, there is no sign of Blackie. Norman's mammy calls, "Normie, lovey, where's your bunny?"

Norman doesn't reply. He is trying to bang out Yankee Doodle, wondering why the pedals won't work. He doesn't see the mangle of black fluff trapped beneath.

146. Something to love and care for.

Ally texts you: hey Greg, U seen the bunny 4 sale on ebay?

You take no notice, the last thing you need is a dumb animal. But the counsellor advised you, 'Get a pet, Greg. Something to love and care for.'

You respond to Ally: where's it at?

No reply. You go on ebay and he's there. A grey lop-eared beauty called Silver. Eyes that speak. You 'buy now' for $10 and bring him home.

You still have your knives. Gleaming. Shining. You remember the thrill of the kill. The first incision.

But this time you can't.

147. Another World

Max strums. Take Me Home, Country Roads. O-mouthed, they sing around the hissing, snapping glowing campfire.

An accidental onlooker might see it as theatre: the orange glow in the young faces; the green aura around their naked bodies; the familiar song in an unfamiliar setting.

Alice frantically reaches for everyone's hands. "Stop," she says, "I don't get it, where's this road? Where is home?"

"That's a different world," they reply, singing another song. About a house called The Rising Sun.

148. After Lights Out

It's your turn to bring the campfire for the dorm's indoor midnight feast. You use your head and bring a light bulb and red tissue paper.

Pity Judy didn't use hers. 'It's not very warm,' she said, striking a match.

At least the firemen were hunky.

149. I am

I am the island
floating thoughts in wells drawn by blindfold donkeys
where St. Paul once walked.

I am aroma memories of Smokey Joe's late night feasts
tinkling laughter clinking glasses upside down on
handkerchiefs
on Father's head. For dancing.

I am snatches of language yassou file mou.
On my tongue lemon soup with wild garlic. A freshening
spring
in the green Morris Minor to the foothills of Kantara.

I am not the Roman tile once picked up from ruins
to become a teapot stand. That was Mother,
who had bad luck, and took it back to Salamis.

I am the fear of moustachioed Eoka gathering
firearms lining the Coca Cola walls in Akhna's cafe
the day I missed the bus.

I am the evacuee who sailed away
across the Mediterranean from my golden island's sun

to dreary grey safety.

I was this place. This taste. This light. This tongue.
Those herbs. Those songs. Those nights.
That time. That understanding. That feeling.

I am.

150. While the Kettle Boils

Herman fills the old copper kettle. He smiles at the memory of his mother's soft advice about freshly drawn water.

The kettle is on the Aga now. He waits, standing, watching. Hearing his mother again, 'Watched kettles…' But what's a guy to do in such a short time? He can't mow the lawn or put up new bookshelves. Surely there is something this old romantic can do.

And so it is that Herman writes his Minute Poem. A poem about something that happens in sixty seconds. With 60 syllables. A poem that can be read in a minute:

Minute Minuet

Rameau's Menuet en Rondeau
for piano
with dancing hands
on keys of gleaming Steinway grands.
Mezzo forte
hear the glory,
pianissimo to gentle
accidentals.

Unrivalled—swift—

that's Rameau's gift.

Herman lays down his pen as he hears the kettle begin to rumble to the boil. The brown teapot is warmed. The boiling water marries with the tea leaves. He breathes in that satisfying aroma of freshly brewed Darjeeling.

In the garden, where the lawn still needs mowing, Herman sits in his mother's rattan chair, his cup of tea beside him on the small glass-topped table. To the backdrop of sweet birdsong, he picks up his poem to read. 'Just think,' he says to no-one, 'I wrote that while the kettle boiled.'

Acknowledgements

My approach to writing short, spontaneous but essential stories is to write, for the most part, without conscious thought. For that approach I must thank Canadian author, playwright and poet, Susan Musgrave whose workshop all those years ago left its mark. It was she who taught me to seek out the essence of a story. Like a good balsamic glaze reduction.

I will always value other literary workshops I've had the good fortune to attend over the years. My thanks to the poet Hugo Williams who drew my attention to line endings, to Donna Morrisey, Barbara Trapido, and Carol Bruneau for steering me towards putting myself in other places, in other skins, in other languages — and then returning to my own. And thanks always to Russell Barton who warned me that taking his creative writing courses twenty years ago would change the way I read any book thereafter. Russell, you were right, I had no idea how much hard work went into bringing a book to a reader.

To my cheerleaders, flag wavers, generous readers and helpers around the world: Jeannie (who said that all important 'Hi' every morning), Alex (for the whippet love), Lesley (for Garibaldis and ukuleles), Mary (for the help with Greek), David, Graham, Norma, Joan (for all your the hearts and thumbs up every time I overcame a hurdle), Jack, Vanessa, and Jude (for the reviews), Natalie, Pam, John, and Alice (for the advice). Thank you.

Thanks to John and Jude at Bath Flash Fiction Ad Hoc for the weekly challenges. Some of these stories would not exist without your prompts.

To the literary journals and magazines around the world that gave my work homes over the years, the best validation an author could ask. Thank you.

A giant thank you goes to my writer family: the members (past and present) of the international online writing group for expats, Writers Abroad. Theirs were the many sets of sharp eyes and minds on this collection before it reached this point. It was they who found the majority of stray apostrophes and sorted out the POVs. These talented and gracious writers gave of their time, expertise and experience—and kept me on my toes. They gave me motivation, support, and close friendships and trust from afar. Some of these stories would not exist without the inspiration of the weekly muse exercises provided by this writing group.

Jack—and by association, Leonard Cohen, who caused my literary corner to turn in 2009. RIP both. Eternal gratitude.

I deeply thank Elke and Kat, for all the afternoon teas sprinkled liberally with literary conversation and good humour. And for their true friendship.

To Jim for the Milliganesque humour that often crept in when I needed it the most, and for your unwavering belief in fairness. Thank you, ta muchly.

Thank yous in bunches and bunches and boat loads of yellow roses go to Vicki for the love, for spotting the over-abundance of Jeds, for always having my back and much more.

To Arne, for your unfailing love and support, for believing in me, thank you for always making all things possible for teaching me that being nosey was just fine. And for knowing the vintage Brylcreem jingle: '…a little dab'll do ya…'

Massive thanks to S.R. Stewart, Kathryn Gerhardt, and all at Unsolicited Press for taking me on, making my collection come alive, and for making the process an absolute joy. And for letting me keep my English spelling.

And finally, thank you to this peaceful corner of the world, where thinking, observing, dreaming and creating can happen.

As a special thanks to you, we would like to offer you an exclusive copy of S.B. Borgersen's novella FISHERMEN'S FINGERS.

Fishermen's Fingers

a novella

S.B. Borgersen

For Elke and Kat
my sounding boards

Author's note

National Novel Writing Month (now known fondly, around the world, as NaNo) is an event where writers of all ages and genres write their hearts out in the thirty days of November. There is no time to plot, write character studies, consider settings, research, edit, rewrite — all of those good disciplines normal to a writer.

No, the idea is to bravely bash out around 2,000 words a day, and to enjoy the liberating feel of writing mostly without conscious thought. Letting the story have its head.

I have done this every November since 2006. *Fishermen's Fingers* is one of three novellas I wrote during NaNo 2018. It was indeed written without conscious thought, this story bears no resemblance to characters or places — it's all fiction.

*

Acknowledgements

To all the good folk at National Novel Writing Month, without your continued commitment to the project, this story would not have been written. To the international writing group, Writers Abroad, your support keeps me motivated and inspired. To the eagle eyes: Kat, Barbara, Chris, Laura, Elke, Kimberly and Pam. I do thank you for your spotting of all my blunders. To wonderful small fishing communities along this coast and to all fisherfolk, who put to sea before dawn in all weathers to put food on tables, you and your families deserve medals for bravery.

To S.R. Stewart and all at Unsolicited Press, you have turned me from a writer into author. Thank you.

And to Arne. You keep our home ticking over through those November writing indulgences, and the rest of the year during my writing hours. Thank you for making all things possible. And for the stories about the pig in the liquor store and the drunk ducks.

Red sky by morning, sailor take warning.
An ancient rhyme often repeated by mariners.

Miss Watson stood before her class of ten-year-olds and moistened her lips. She needed to warn them. It was her job. She looked at their faces of innocence, at their lack of street-wisdom, at their trust and acceptance in every member of the fishing community. She looked at the empty chair on the back row. She began to tell them about Betty. And why she wasn't in school today.

Chapter 1

BETTY SITS ON the bank contemplating her parents' discussion around the table last night. She kicks at the skeleton. She knows it was a porcupine from the shower of quills along the gravel edge. She toes the curved spine, perfect in its formation and wonders what kind of brain was once in that small skull.

Alongside the spread of bones is an unmoving chickadee. "Must've been hit by something," the ten-year-old murmurs, reaching down to stroke its minute head of still-silky but dead feathers. She touches its beak, smaller than a grain of corn.

Betty remembers last night's heated talk then. About the poor crop. How there'll be no money for anything. How Ma said she'll go back out West and take Betty with her.

How Pa said, "Over my dead body."

There's peanut butter sandwiches for supper, "Ain't no money for more," says Ma, but gives Betty a sideways grin, "Lift the corner of the tablecloth," she whispers, "when Pa goes out to the tavern."

Betty's not stupid, she knows the correlation between not enough money for food and Pa going to the tavern but keeps her own counsel. She's learned well from the best; her ma, who learned from her own mother. That was before Nanny went to jail for shooting Kenny who wouldn't let her play the spoons in Hank's band—but that's a whole 'nother story.

It is past six o'clock before Pa leaves and Betty is getting real anxious to lift the corner of the oil cloth with its faded blue flowers among the rubbed-off green. But as Pa swings his rough brown coat from the peg by the back kitchen door, she is ready with her mouth watering.

Ma has left her the latest copy of the story book magazine Betty collects. This week there is a free notebook inside the packet too and a small red ready-sharpened pencil. 'Write Your Own Story,' it says on the cover of the magazine. On the front of the notebook it says, 'My Story by dot-dot-dot.' That is the place for Betty to write her own name.

She wonders if she should use a pseudonym—she knows what that is — just in case people recognise themselves in her book and come after her. 'Nom-de-Plume' is what her teacher, Miss Watson, called it. 'French' she'd said. 'Pen Name.' Betty liked that idea and carefully printed on the cover of the notebook. 'Elizabeth James.' She'd heard that sometimes lady authors take their husband's first names as their nom-de-plume last name. And as Betty's full name is Elizabeth and as she dreams her one-day husband will be James, then Elizabeth James had the most perfect ring to it. That's what Betty thinks anyway.

Chapter 2

THE NELLY-MAY PULLS away at dawn. The bay is flat-ass calm and 'I'll be at the traps before the rest of 'em,' thinks Lenny as he lets the Nelly-May have her head. She's an aging lobster boat and belonged to an old man, that was Murray, the only person to ever really believe in Lenny. To give him a chance. The licence and boat got willed to Lenny when Murray died. That's how they did it then.

He sees the sun come up — well part of the sun. There's an eclipse today and for Lenny that could mean trouble. He knows he has problems working stuff out, but this eclipse is something else and he understands it. The sun rises above the horizon like a red scimitar, blade pointing off at 2 o'clock. The absolute stillness gives him a chill, he's felt it before, years before when he's done things he later knew he shouldn't.

Like taking young Florrie Henderson into the woods and making her take off her knickers while he watched. Drooling, playing with himself. Watching her shiver and sob like a small defenceless animal. He didn't touch her. Not once, just himself until oh joy, he came onto the soft carpet of moss, over and over, while she shut her eyes and held tight to her pigtails as if they would pull her out of her nightmare.

When he was done he told her, "Sort yerself out you wicked child," and dropped her back on the hauling road so she could walk home, "say anything and I'll tell about your wickedness," he said.

He heard no more, Florrie's mother came to the wharf often when the boats were coming in and bought lobster from him. Never said a word. So it must've been OK. Florrie was sent away soon after, he heard, to a special hospital for the nervous. Well, she were a bit edgy, again he tells himself, if only she'd just stood still and let him see without him having to be so bossy, she needn't have cried like that. He didn't much like the look of her dirty knickers either. Dirty child.

There'd not been an eclipse since then — not here anyway — 1993 was it? he can't remember. That dirty little Florrie must be all growed up now. At least twenty anyway. He doesn't know what happened to the rest of the family. Moved away, they said. Lenny felt nothing when he heard that. It was nothing.

There have been times when he'd needed dirty little Florrie and was pissed off that she'd been sent away. He wouldn't have given her a two-dollar bill if he'd known she wouldn't be around for long. Money wasted.

There is a stillness over the water that is uncanny. No sign of life at all. No other boat as the water turns from peach to purple to aquamarine. No dolphins breaking the water, no sharks, no whales. He sits back in the wheelhouse with his first beer and unzips his pants.

Chapter 3

IT'S 'SHOW AND TELL' at school today. Chrissy has brought in the teddy bear her nanny has made for her. It is knitted in yellow itchy wool with a black stitched nose and purple buttons for eyes. They've been stitched on with green wool that make crosses. The kids laugh and Chrissy is about to cry when Miss Watson produces balls of yarn and knitting needles for everyone.

She puts one ball and two needles before each child. "Now how do you make an animal out of those?" she says.

Everyone looks at her with open mouths and even wider eyes. Todd Matthews holds up his hands. "We could take them to Chrissy's nanny for her to show us," he says.

"Good suggestion Todd, but no," says Miss Watson, "we will begin to learn ourselves. Together."

She shows the children how to make the first stitch by putting a loop over the needle and tying it in a loose knot. They all copy her. She walks around the classroom, checking that they've done it before continuing with 'binding on' as she calls it. This is where they need to add 9 more stitches to the needle to make ten in total, by using their thumbs, they loop the yarn over the needle, pull it not too tight, then continue on.

She has to put a few back on track. Ronny has let his ball of yarn fall and roll across the classroom floor picking up dust and grit as it makes its way between the table legs, but Betty picks it up under hers and begins to wind it, hands it back down the line until it's back with Ronny. He grins and waves his needles in the air.

"You must always respect your knitting needles," says Miss Watson. "Rule numero uno."

The children all laugh. Miss Watson often uses interesting ways of reminding them of things. Numero uno means it is important and they all remember that.

As they sit with ten stitches on their left-hand needle, she continues to show them how to knit a row. One stitch at a time, "Just like life," she says, "one step at a time, a good life lesson."

The children count out loud as they knit their first row. Ronny finishes last. But at least he finishes after getting mixed up around 7 and 8. He finishes with a, "Whoop - TEN."

The class applaud him. Miss Watson gives him a button for his achievement. "When you've finished making your animal," she says, "this will be his first eye. The animal will be what?"

She looks up at the class. They look at the ten stitches on their knitting needle. "Not a teddy bear then?" says Ronny.

Miss Watson opens her desk and brings out a scarlet sausage dog. It has black as coal button eyes and little dumpy legs. The class all gasp in unison, like when the school bus slows down with that unique noise.

"The piece we've started with is a leg, we have to make four of them before we do a body and a head."

"And a tail," calls out Betty from the back row.

The class cheer because Betty doesn't always say too much.

Miss Watson hands Ronny a bright blue button. She tells him that it will go perfectly for his sausage dog in his pale green yarn. "He will be a blue-eyed puppy dog," she says, "you'll need to give him a name."

The rest of the class then go forward to Miss Watson's desk to pick out their own first button. Betty picks black for her pink sausage dog which will be a girl puppy.

"Now keep your eye buttons very safe," says Miss Watson. "And put your needles and yarn in your backpacks, safely at the bottom. Take them home but bring them back on Monday. Now we'll have our Friday afternoon story."

Chapter 4

LENNY LEANS AGAINST the bar. The tavern smells of old fish, wet woollen clothing, tobacco of many kinds, and talk that would make their grandfathers blush.

But for Lenny it's where he feels most at home. There's a comfort in the smells. It is dark and woody. The bottles don't shine too bright. Everything has an amber glow to it when he's had a few pulls on his weed. And all is right with his world.

He guesses people know that he has weaknesses. He's only been arrested a few times and only because of people's complaints, he has never been charged. Kept in the jail overnight a few times which has never bothered him. He gets a free meal and to watch TV which he can't normally do as he doesn't have one himself.

There is one in the tavern but it's usually set to the sports channel, sometimes the news. Lenny isn't interested in sports unless it is darts. And he doesn't give a shit for the news — he says the media folks are manipulative. A word he has picked up recently when listening to some of the women shopping in the grocery store. They'd been talking about the president of America.

Lenny doesn't give a chickadee's dick for America. Or for politics either. But he keeps his own council until he's had a few more beers and rum chasers. Then he lets it all out and look out anyone who's around then. Sparks will fly and Lenny's language is off the wall.

But for now he leans against the bar and thinks about his day. How he watched all the little kids come out of school with their book bags. How they clambered up the high steps onto the school buses. How he wishes he could have helped lift them up, especially the little girls. With their pink tee shirts and tight leggings around their tight little bums. He thinks about what they have for bum cracks. And how he'd like to wiggle his fingers there and then taste them.

"Another one Lenny?"

"Wha…?"

"Beer?"

"Yup," he says with no manners. They know he doesn't use manners at all and accept him for what he his — or what they think he is.

He wants to knock this beer back and head out to the other side of the bridge. Where the school bus turns. Where the last of the little kids get off and saunter back to their nice warm kitchens with their wood stoves and their moms having milk and cookies all ready for them. Where they'll turn out their homework onto the kitchen table and their loving moms will lean over and point out what they should write.

Lenny never had a mom like that. And he never rode a school bus. In his day you walked from the orphans' home to school in all weathers rain or shine. You got there and had to bring wood in for the stove, empty the slop bucket before you even learned to write your own name. He hated school. Hated the teacher who used a cane to whack them for the slightest thing. That man struck Lenny every day. Every day he promised that one day he would get him.

He was thirteen when he cut the brake cables of the teacher's car. When the guy disappeared into the lake that was the water supply, drowning in the ice and algae, "Good for 'im," Lenny told himself.

No-one was ever held responsible. 'Came off in the ice on the bend, accidental death,' they'd said.

"Good riddance," said Lenny.

But the damage was done. Lenny was broken as a child and from then on was a broken man filled with badness that no-one could repair even if they'd known. Some said a good woman would sort him out. But what good woman would want anything to do with the snarly man who didn't take care of himself? Never bathed or shaved. Never washed his clothes and got all of his nutrition at the tavern, or his weed supplier or at the still he'd set up himself in the middle of the wooded land that he'd won years before in a bet.

It was a lucky bet really. Lenny came in right at the end and the other guys had turned to him and said, "What card do you think it is Lenny?" Lenny had picked out the Jack of Spades. The result: 28 acres of dense woodland with a single-track laneway leading in. He'd let the laneway get overgrown so no-one would ever find it. Never find him, if he ever wanted to take himself off for a bit.

And never find out what he really got up to when he wasn't out fishing.

Chapter 5

BETTY IS FILLED with excitement about her knitting project and rushes off the bus and through the gate at the entrance to their farm lane. She's wearing her pink rain boots, which is just as well as the farm lane is muddy most of the time.

Her mother is baking molasses cookies, if there is one thing Betty likes more than ice cream, it is molasses cookies. She smells the ginger and the brown sugar as her mother adds to the eggs and flour. She watches, her mouth watering, as her mother spoons the batter onto the cookie sheet.

"Ten minutes," says Ma, "they'll be hot, but if you start your homework you can have two, one for each hand."

Betty thinks this is a perfect day all around and empties her backpack onto the kitchen table. Out rolls the ball of yarn and the knitting needles.

"Ooooh," says Ma. "You're learning to knit, good for Miss Watson, it is a good thing to learn you know, I knitted for years until my arthritis took over. You'll let me do a little, won't you?"

Betty nods. Slowly as if she's not sure she should let Ma do her homework. But she's excited to make her sausage dog and counts slowly as she knits her first row at home. "One... two... three..."

"What will it be?" says Ma.

"It's a sausage dog," says Betty, "Ma, what really is a sausage dog, is it like a hot dog?"

"In a ways," says Ma, "I think that's why the hot dogs are called Weiners. A Weiner is a German dog that has a long body like a sausage, and four little legs. We had one once when I was little. His name was Solly, I don't know why. My ma named him I think when Pa brought him home. Pa won him in a raffle or something. maybe something to do with a card party he was at."

"Can I call mine Solly too?" says Betty. "Can it be a girl's name? My sausage dog will be a girl."

"I don't see why not," says Ma. "People use all kinds of names now, just look at pop singers."

Betty hums along with her knitting, "four...five...six... what a pretty Solly you will be."

Chapter 6

LENNY IS AT the tavern talking to Chrissy at the tavern's side-line pizza counter. "My poppy had a pig once," he said. Chrissy takes little notice of Lenny. She's well aware Lenny has no family whatsoever. That he makes things up to entertain, to get free pizzas and beer.

"He was at the liquor store with his brother Mel. They'd just bought the pig. A baby pig it was."

"That's a piglet," says Chrissy who finished her grade 12 before working at the pizza counter.

"Right," says Lenny, "a piglet then. Cute little thing it was, I was maybe seven or eight years old myself."

"Piglet," says Chrissy, under her breath.

"Anyhow," says Lenny, they took the little pig into the liquor store with them, they didn't want to leave it in the back of the truck, case someone stole it."

"Right," says Chrissy, aware that the rest of the clientele were listening in to Lenny's story now.

"Pops, and his brother, my Uncle Mel were drunk as always."

"Ya don't say," says Chrissy, rolling her eyes, but aware that the story was holding the interests of the entire pizza place.

"Well, by the Jesus didn't the little pig get loose in the liquor store," says Lenny, cracking a grin, showing his brown teeth. Eyes shining as the folks began clapping.

"You should have seen them," he cackled, "Pops and Uncle Mel chasing around the aisles of rum, the little pig running faster than either of them, squealing at them."

The folks round the pizza counter were laughing out loud now, cheering and clapping. "Buy the man a beer," says someone.

"Right," says Chrissy, "s'pose it's worth it for a laugh." she pours a tall glass of cold Coors Lite. Lenny's eyes light up even brighter. "I have more stories about the old days," he says. "Shall I save them for another time?"

"You do that Lenny," says Chrissy, rolling her eyes, as she pushes the glass towards him, wondering if she'll need to disinfect it when he's gone.

Chapter 7

"CAN I GO outside and play?" says Betty. "I've done one whole row Mom, that's ten whole stitches."

Chapter 8

LENNY IS IN the coffee shop. He orders a Boston Cream doughnut and a double-cream, double-sugar, coffee. He removes the lid immediately and takes it to a seat in the far corner, away from the gaggle of giggling white curly-headed shoppers. He's no time for these gossipy women and he knows full well how they don't like him, with his raggedy beard and his long greasy hair. His dirty fishy clothes and black fingernails.

He slurps his coffee and his old friend Billy joins him. Billy in his dirty donated jeans. 'Birds-of-a-feather,' whisper the gaggle of grey-haired grannies in the opposite corner before getting back to their knitting and their current victim of gossip.

"You told 'em the story of the pig, I hear," says Billy. "You haven't told that one for some time."

Lenny grunts. "I don't know what kicked me off," he says, "but you know what folks are like, everyone sinking into their beer, no-one talking, thought it might liven things up a bit."

"You should tell the one about the choke cherry wine and the ducks next time," says Billy, "They'd like that, especially in the tavern."

"You remember that?" says Lenny.

"Sure do," says Billy, "I could've bin there miself, seen the ducks all laying on their backs with their webby feet in the air, happy as pigs in muck."

"It did for them though, din it?" says Lenny. "All those poor ducks went into someone's supper that week. Apparently they tasted good, very moist and not one bit fatty."

Billy nods. He remembers now. It was his story really, he'd told it to Lenny, how his ma was angry at the boys. How they'd filtered off the wine and were told to take the remnants, all the bits left over and put them in the burn barrel. How they'd done no such thing. How they'd tipped all the old berry skins out onto the lawn in back of the house, laughed and run into the barn to watch through the tiny broken window as the ducks waddled out. Cackling with excitement at a new treat.

"You wus just kids though," says Lenny. "You didn't know them ducks 'd git drunk, did ya?"

Billy nods. Then shakes his head. It's a Billy thing. Generous with giving Lenny his stories. But he's a fence sitter. He'll answer yes and no to most all things. He did get into trouble that day. Got a good beating from his father. Those ducks were to be the family's income for Christmas. They had orders for ducks that year and it would be another month before they were ready to be killed and sold. Now there would be nothing.

Lenny remembers Billy first telling him about that Christmas. How here wasn't much. Potatoes and turnip for dinner. That's about all. He'd hoped for a trumpet. Wanted to play like Louis Armstrong. He'd practiced his voice over and over, got the growl just about right.

But Billy never did get a trumpet. Never learned to play an instrument. He'd only ever told Lenny about his time as a boy. The only time Lenny ever saw him with a tear in his crusty eyes.

Lenny saunters out of the coffee shop, kicking at stones like a ten-year-old would. He is sixty and never been loved, not really loved. And never had anyone to love in return.

He sees young Betty playing in her front yard in her pink boots. He leans over the fence. "Hi Sweetie," he calls.

"Go 'way," she says, "Ma says I mustn't talk to strange men."

"I'm no stranger Sweetie, am I? I'm a good friend to your old uncle Billy."

"Oh," says Betty, "s'pose that's OK then. I'm learning to knit," she says, being polite as her mother always told her. "I'm knitting a sausage dog at school. That's a dacksoond or something," she says.

"Do you want to see some real puppies?" says Lenny. "I can take you and show you."

Betty hesitates. Then she hears her mother calling her in for supper. She leaves Lenny at the fence, "See ya," she says, to be friendly. She waves and Lenny sees her little pink boots plip-plop across the muddy lawn and into the back kitchen of the house he has never been allowed into.

Billy pulls over in his beat up old Dodge. "Ya wanna come?" he says.

"Where ya goin'," says Lenny.

"Liquor store," say Billy. "They are opening today for cannabis."

"Right with ya," says Lenny, "Mebbe I'll git me some."

It is the first day of the Cannabis Act. It has caused somewhat of a stir with users, dealers, non users and the medical profession.

Lenny and Billy park the truck what seems like miles from the normal parking lot. The line-up at the liquor store is right around the block. Some folks are still in their pyjamas. Some are in shorts with bare chests. It is October. That's still summer for some folk. There are people in business suits. There are women in stiletto heels. It is a complete cross-section of humanity.

By the time Lenny and Billy get to the counter which is in a separate section with a toll gate inside the liquor store, there is not much left. "We have the oils," says the clerk. "What do you need the cannabis for?"

"This ain't a question we've ever bin axed," says Billy in his best voice, trying to stop two of his teeth falling out of his rotten mouth. "We just like it."

Lenny says, quite out of the blue, "For pain, for relaxation when we're stressed."

"The oil is best," says the clerk, "you can order it online."

Billy looks at Lenny. "On Line. Dja know what that is?"

"Here, says the clerk. I'll show you." She walks around to the client side of the counter and opens up her screen.

"Ahh like TV," says Billy.

"I'll give you a card with a number," says the clerk, as it dawns on her that she's fighting a losing battle with these two. "If you go to the library, or even a school computer lab, they can show you how. Well, maybe not a school, you have to be over nineteen, so there'll be no computer access there." she adds.

Billy and Lenny return to the truck each with a little plastic card with a scratch panel on the back. Apparently, they've been told that is their unique number with which they can order online.

"Well, that weren't much good, were it?" says Billy.

Lenny nods as Billy shakes his head. "Let's go to the tavern," says Lenny, "we don't need to go to a computer for that."

Chapter 9

BETTY AND RONNY got married last year, both twenty-two and both so sure of what they each wanted. Needed.

Ronny brings Betty breakfast in bed. Toast with her favourite marmalade made by his mother each winter. They have to make six bottles last a year — "that's yer quota," Ronny's Ma told them, so go easy. "If you want to make marmalade cakes, you'll have to get it from the grocery store."

It's not been easy for Ronny. He helped Betty through her trauma from when she was ten years old.

She still doesn't say much about it. But she hangs on to her little pink sausage dog that she was making at the time. He is pink with brown eyes. The black buttons were lost in the mud. Miss Watson had the rest of the class share in the finishing of Betty's sausage dog after Betty was found back in the woods by the big rocks. When all they'd found to start with was the ball of yarn. It was the ball of yarn that led the search party to her. Crouched beneath a rock. Unable to speak. Unable to cry out. Unable to move.

Beside her was Lenny. Blood congealed across his face. One of Betty's knitting needles sticking from his eye. The other from his throat. Billy sitting beside him, crying like a baby.

The search crew had never seen anything like it. They all had counselling afterwards that went on for weeks. Betty's counsellor tried in vain to get Betty to talk.

But she never has.

Ronny spreads the marmalade for her. The toast is just how she likes it, with real butter, not Becel. Her doctor has monitored her progress and Betty has responded well, but twelve years. Twelve years of nightmares. Twelve years of learning to trust. Twelve years of Uncle Billy still coming to visit Ma and Pa.

Betty immersed herself in learning very soon after it all happened. Home schooling was not an option so Miss Watson visited three times a week and set Betty assignments. Guiding her through a curriculum that would set her up for university.

The community held fund raisers. What happened was on the conscience of many townsfolk. 'We should have seen the signs,' they said. 'We could have done something…'

And so, funds were raised. Betty sailed through all the academic grounding for college. The funds were there to see her through for at least three years.

But in the end, she hadn't the confidence to leave her home, her family, and the love that had grown with Ronny.

Miss Watson retired round about the same time, and so together they pursued a correspondence degree course, using the computer and once a semester travelling to the city for tutorials.

Chapter 10

THE MORNING OF Lenny's funeral is dank and dark. A storm's been brewing through the night and hurricane force winds are in the forecast. Folks have been warned of power cuts and told to fill their kettles and bathtubs with water, and charge anything that can be recharged.

The funeral is not at the church. But in the back room of the tavern. "Seems right, somehow," says Billy.

Others agreed, although no-one really knew Lenny like Billy. But Billy's footing the bill for this, "Least I can do," he mutters as other folks in the town glower at him. "The guy was not all bad."

No-one nods. Billy nods and shakes his head, as only Billy can, and appears on the stroke of 11 o'clock in a rumpled grey suit he's picked up at the thrift store. He wears an off-white shirt with a collar. And a tie. Albeit a polyester tie with a picture of a naked woman down the front. "The only one left at the thrift store," he says, when one of the guys says, "Well Lenny would certainly approve of that."

There is no official music, but Danny behind the bar switches on 100.7 which is playing Willy Nelson's *Blue Eyes Crying in the Rain*. Turns out the entire morning is given over to Willie Nelson. Billy reckons he couldn't have organized it any better if he'd tried.

Lenny is in a purple plastic container on the bar. His ashes anyway. Danny places a ring of rum shot glasses around the ashes. As Willie begins *By the Rivers of Babylon* the assembled company lift their tot of rum and say, "To Lenny, RIP."

The morning turns into the afternoon and the rains come down like someone hosing the town from a thousand fire trucks. The power flickers. The guys are ready with their counting. It flickers the second time. They know that a third means the power will go out. And could do for days.

They sit in darkness and in silence. Danny reaches for the 40-ouncer of rum and refills the glasses. Billy has had lobster rolls made up and they are still in a large Amazon box in the stock room. He takes Danny's flashlight and brings them out. "Fill yer boots," he says. "The lobster's on Lenny. This was his final haul."

By six o'clock as the waters rose the funeral party was in full swing in spite of no power. Out came the cards and the dollars were flying fast and furiously. Nobody mentioned Lenny after a while, and Billy nodded to himself, then shook his head, not deciding on whether this was a good thing, or a bad. He supposed that what they'd done was given Lenny a good send off. Better than a pyre on the Nelly-May in the middle of the bay, which is how Lenny had once described the way he wanted to go.

Chapter 11

LENNY WATCHES FROM his rusting brown Dodge Dakota truck at the end of the laneway. He sees the little pink boots tottering around in the mud, he looks up to see Betty's sweet face. She is ten but looks more like seven or eight everyone says. She's still in her own yard, splashing up and down the once gravelled pathway. She smiles, her ponytail bobs up and down just like a pony's would trotting around a green field on a sunny day.

Only today looks like more rain. The dark clouds on the horizon are so familiar to Lenny. He always knows when, and when not, to take out the Nelly-May. When it comes to his boat Lenny takes no chances. Unlike now. He pulls on his smoke, the last of his weed, and the last of his money to get more. It makes him antsy when he's got neither one nor the other.

He fidgets in the truck. The cracked plastic seats irritate him. The smeary windshield irritates him and he gets that uncontrollable urge in his groin.

He watches Betty more closely. She hasn't got breasts yet, 'probably a late developer,' he tells himself. 'Not like those other brazen girls in her same grade at middle school, they bounce up and down like young maidens on a mountain side.' He has no idea where that turn of phrase has come from other than he once saw The Sound of Music on a TV in a store window. Saw the pictures, but with no sound. All he saw were maidens' breasts jigging up and down with the mountains behind.

The drizzle eases off and he climbs out of the truck. At the same time Betty opens the garden gate, she sees Lenny and politely says, "Hi, how are you?" Not waiting for his reply.

He calls back, "Fine and dandy, young lady, I'm off to see how my puppies are making out. Wanna come along?"

Betty hesitates, thinks about what her mother has told her about strangers. But Lenny is not a stranger is he? He's a friend of Uncle Billy and she has spoken with him before a few times now, so he is no stranger.

"OK," she says, "I'll just tell my ma in case she worries."

Betty runs into the house, her little pink boots plopping up and down along the muddy garden path.

Lenny gets a lump in his throat, not just in his nether regions and returns to the truck, climbs in and hopes Betty's mother says, 'no.'

But here she comes, little Betty with her little pink boots, and shining pink face filled with expectation and anticipation. His heart leaps and then sinks. She climbs into the truck with difficulty. "You OK?" he says.

"Yup," she says, "I can do it."

"What ya ma say?"

"Can't find her, she must've gone to the store for more butter, she's making a cake for my birthday tomorrow."

"Your birthday tomorrow?" asks Lenny, "How old?"

"I'll be ten," she says, puffed up with pride, her ponytail swinging. Lenny notices the little pink plastic butterfly that holds her ponytail in place. He swallows hard.

"Puppies?"

"Yes, please," she says, remembering her manners. "How old are they?"

Lenny is caught out by the question. Has to think very hard. "Six weeks," he says, off the cuff.

"They must be so tiny then, what kind?"

Again, Lenny is stumped. He doesn't know dog breeds that well other than Duck Tollers. So that's what he says, "Tollers, Nova Scotia Duck Tollers, the colour of taffy"

Betty settles down on the bench seat of the truck beside Lenny. The old crocheted afghan thrown over the back stinks of tobacco and weed, she knows the smell. There's also the smell of booze and that she doesn't like. It was booze that caused her pa to leave home. To leave her and her ma to struggle without him.

"Actually," she says, "can we just stop at the store, I want to get some candy first."

Lenny's heart lifts at the thought of candy and has no problem pulling in at the curb by the FoodMart.

Betty doesn't come out for the longest time. He wonders why. Through his smeary windshield he sees Betty talking to her mother. And he knows he is probably in the shit.

He moves on without switching on his motor. He rolls the truck out into the road on neutral as he has done on many occasions and then starts her up. He heads for the tavern, something, anything, to take away the longing. Surely someone there will buy him a beer.

"Whatcha doin' Lenny," Billy calls to him down the length of the bar, "Wanna beer?"

Lenny is glad that his panic is over. He never gives a thought to the fact that things happen in his head and with his crotch over which he has no control. But knows beer with Billy will go a long way to quenching everything. He puts the frothing bottle back on the bar after a swig and says, "Back in a bit."

In the gents washroom he wanks off to feel better. Doesn't feel one bit better, in fact feels fucking miserable, but puts on a brave face and goes back to Billy at the bar. The other guys have gathered around, "I told them you'd have more stories," says Billy.

"Not today guys, sorry," says Lenny. "Maybe tomorrow. Unless of course each story is worth a beer."

That works, they perch on bar stools and lean against the bar as Lenny begins, "My ole pa 'ad a still, ya know," the guys all nod, as if they really do know, but no-one had a clue that Lenny had no idea if he had a father, or who he might be.

Lenny's ma was just a young girl around fifteen when she had Lenny. He was born in the back of old Gordie Levi's barn. Behind a bale of hay with the goats chewing at one end of the bale. Lenny's ma (no-one knew her name then) was not a fragile little thing, no, a robust girl with legs like tree trunks and a bosom like the rocky mountains, so legend had it. She shelled out the baby, a boy, stuck him to her breast where he latched right on and guzzled.

Once she'd given him a good feed, she'd wrapped him in a towel she'd plucked from some old washing line and left him in the barn with the goats.

Old Gordie Levi found him that night and took him into the kitchen where his wife, Ada, was just serving up the turnip stew for their supper.

"What in the hell have you there, Gordie?" she squarked.

"It's a goddamm babby, can't you see woman, can't you hear?"

Lenny was screaming his little lungs out at this point and Ada said, "Gimme here," she dipped her finger in a bowl of milk warming on the Enterprise stove all ready for making Gordie's nightly coffee, and the baby suckled.

"We canna keep him ya know," said Gordie.

Ada, knew this, she'd never had children. Never had anything but Gordie and all his animals to take care of. A baby had eluded her and here she was over sixty years old. Childless, and no-one to look after them in their old age.

"We'll hand him in in the morning," said Gordie.

The couple sat up with the baby all night, Ada dipping her little finger into the warm milk every so often. They wrapped him in a shawl that Ada's mother had knitted years before, when Ada and Gordie got married, thinking there was sure to be a baby on the way soon after. It didn't happen, but Ada had kept the shawl in the cedar trunk all these forty years or more.

"What will we say?" she said to Gordie.

"Well, the truth of course," said Gordie, "how we found him in the barn."

Constable Brown at the station took one look at the screwed up little newborn at 7.30 the next morning and slowly wrote out their statement. "We'll get it to the hospital in the city," he said.

"Him," said Ada, "it is a baby boy…"

"Right," said Constable Brown. "A boy. What should we call him?"

"We called him Leonard last night," said Gordiie. "If we'd ever had a son, we'd have called him Leonard."

"Do you want that back?" Constable Brown held up the fine lace shawl.

"Ada?"

"Well," said Ada, "I guess not, we've no use for it now, the wee mite needs something to wrap around him."

As they walk down the wet grey steps of the police station, Gordie takes Ada's arm, "We couldn't keep him you know," he says.

"'I know," she says, "if only we'd been 20 years younger, then…"

"Even then," said Gordie. "Even then, it wouldn't be right."

They never saw the child again. Often they wondered as they sat by the stove, keeping their toes warm in the winter. But they hoped he'd get a good home and be loved, as they might well have loved him.

Chapter 12

LENNY FINGERS THE piece of rag in his pocket. It is grey with age. And fragile too. His rough hands catch in the fine wool. There have been times when he could have thrown it out. But something always stopped him.

Maybe Billy calling up the track, "Hurry up Lenny, I've been waiting for you," when they've been going to snare rabbits. Or when his truck broke down, as it often did and he'd looked for a rag to wipe his oily greasy hands, the piece of lace would find its way into his clutches and then he'd say, "Nah," and push it back in his pocket — right to the bottom of his pocket as if to say, "stop popping up, stop haunting me, stop reminding me."

Because without knowing it, the piece of rag was the only thing Lenny had from his past. He sometimes held it to his nose. He imagined he could smell hay. Or goats. One thing he could not smell was a mother.

He tries to forget the home for outcast children. The cold. The hard work in the fields from dawn until dark. The leather strap if you didn't yield enough blueberries, or cranberries, or whatever it was they'd been sent out to gather and pick and collect for the higher-ups to make money.

He was fourteen when he cut his way through the fence with a pair of stolen wire cutters. He still has those somewhere in his truck. They are another reminder of where he came from. He has no recollection of anyone kind. No smiling face. No gentle touch. The harshness seems unfair to him now somehow when he sees how other people treat their children. Even those kids with only a mother. Or only a father.

Lenny just longs for a gentle touch. Someone to stroke his forehead when the headaches come on. The blinding headaches that send him into a rage. Just a tender touch from a tender hand.

He has never had a girlfriend, or woman friend for that matter, much as he has tried. There was a girl, Alexa, who said, "Clean your act up Lenny, and I might be interested."

But he didn't understand. He thought she meant something totally different, that he had to act a part or some such thing. He did try cleaning his teeth with spruce gum once, like the first nations people used to do, he was told, but that just left horrible black stickiness in his mouth and so he needed a joint to take all of that away. And one joint would follow another and he never saw Alexa after that.

Billy got a girlfriend. Lenny was totally pissed off that he went off with a woman called Ginny or something, short for Virginia, Billy told him.

"Is she?" said Lenny.

"Is she what?" said Billy.

"You know," said Lenny. "A virgin. Never been fucked."

Billy kicked him in the balls at that comment before replying. "I don't know and I'll not tell you when I find out either."

Chapter 13

"STILL NO REPLY?" says Ada.

"Nothing," says Gordie, "nothing in the mailbox. We'll probably never hear what really happened to the little fellow."

"They did give you the right address?"

"Yes. I'm pretty sure it's the one Constable Brown gave us. We'll try again next month."

"OK," she says, "I have his birthday card to mail, he'll be four."

Chapter 14

BILLY STANDS AT the small memorial in the town centre. It is November the 11th and everywhere is closed, 'as it should be,' Billy thought.

It is a while since Lenny passed over. Billy still misses his funny friend. The guy he'd known pretty much all his life. Billy places his poppy on the cement that the memorial stands on. There is only one other. That's besides the wreath placed by the mayor on behalf of the town. 'A pretty raggedy thing,' thinks Billy, 'probably made in China.'

He wonders who has placed the other poppy. It is there before the right time and no one normally places anything before 11 am. Billy has stood on the opposite side of the road beside the closed farmers market for at least half an hour waiting, needing a pee really, but waiting regardless.

And he hasn't seen anyone. Other than the person in a green car, a Pontiac, he thinks, slow down, and pause, as if in respect and reflection. Billy had thought nothing of it, it was all quite normal really, but then, maybe that is where the other poppy had come from.

He picks it up. There is a little sticker on the back. *In memory of my baby*, it says, *I should never have let you go.*

That's a mystery for Billy. Does it mean Lenny, his friend Lenny? Or is it someone who went away to war and didn't come back. 'That must be it,' thinks Billy, 'it cannot be for Lenny.'

Chapter 15

HER NAME IS Frannie. She lives in the city with her granddaughter now. In a big house with a grand back yard with lawns and rhododendrons and arbours with climbing roses in the summer. A pool for koi and water plants and a gentle trickling waterfall. Frannie often sits beside the pool, even in cooler weather, looking at her own reflection, seeing the young fifteen-year-old that she was.

She sees the barn where he was born. She hears his cries still now after all these years. It wrenched her heart out then and still does.

Her granddaughter, Eleanor, had helped her trace what happened. Using the internet. It took months of careful crosschecking. Eleanor kept copious and detailed notes.

There was one hand written slip of paper from a police station, with a scant report by a constable, stating that an elderly couple had brought in the baby that had been left as a newborn in their barn. Eleanor and Frannie have their names and the name of the community. She imagines if they were elderly then, they would be long gone from this earth. But still, the name of the community is there. In black and white.

She is horrified to find that her little boy had been placed in care right from day one really, as soon as he was well enough to leave the hospital.

She'd visited the hospital a few weeks ago, walked the halls. Imagined the care her boy had received.

But she hadn't visited the homes he'd been put into. Institutionalised right from a few days old. She cannot forgive herself.

Eleanor discovered that, as an adult, the boy, as a young man, had moved back to the original community and become a fisherman. With a boat, the Nelly-May. Frannie took comfort in that thought and with her granddaughter planned to visit, to seek him out. To say sorry.

The death notice in the archived paper caught them both with a jolt. It happened months before their planned visit. "Too late," weeps Frannie, "just too little too late."

"Grannie, do not cry," says Eleanor. "We can still go. One day we will go anyway."

"I often wondered if he would try and find me," she said. "Obviously not. Maybe he just hated me."

"So many if-onlies in this world," says Eleanor.

Frannie pulls her close and kisses her forehead. "Indeed," she says, "if only we knew what the future held. I just hope he was loved. But it doesn't really look like it."

"Grannie, I've never asked you before, but what about his father?"

Frannie swallows so hard she feels like she might choke. "He was a bad man," she says. "A very very bad man. I just hope my boy took after me. And not him."

Chapter 16

LENNY RAN AWAY from the home at fourteen. A lean and hungry looking boy just beginning to get fuzz over his top lip and on his chin. He'd picked up a cocky swagger with his walk and always had his hands in his pockets.

He wore his scars like a secret though. The welts across his back from the repeated beatings at all the homes he'd been in. All, mostly, for standing up for himself and others. For asking for clean sheets for another boy who repeatedly wet the bed and was repeatedly beaten for it. Lenny got the beatings, too. Lashings across his back, leaving scars that would only be seen if he ever showed them to someone. Or if he was in an accident of some kind.

And he did think as he got older that he was heading for an accident. The way the masters and matrons at the home told him, "You're a bad 'un alright young Lenny, you'll get your come-uppance."

'Well, now they can get their come-uppance,' he told himself as he stole out through the dark midnight corridors, pockets filled with thieved coins and paper money too from the office. The place he'd come to know. The place with the padded doors so no-one would hear the screams and cries of beatings.

He'd taken it all in each time he'd been bent over the sawhorse to get eight or ten lashings, depending on just what he'd done. Or what was said he'd done.

Between gasps he'd noticed where drawers and cupboards were, where keys hung on hooks, and he even manufactured misdemeanours in order to glean as much information as he could.

He stuffed a pillowcase with as many clothes as would fit: socks and shirts. No underwear. The boys in this home didn't wear underwear, all the easier for the masters to beat their bare flesh he supposed. It might have saved on washing too, but washing was not uppermost in his mind as he wove his way down hallways and stepped through the big barred heavy wooden doors with their iron bolts.

Once clear he ran for all his worth to the far woods and then through the fields beyond. He'd seen the envelopes in the office addressed to him. Letters that he'd never been given. Letters he'd asked for and been beaten for asking. He knew someone was trying to find him.

And he noted the town on the postmark. And that was where he was heading.

Chapter 17

BETTY SINGS AS she skips the garden path. Her mother watches through the kitchen window. She knows the song that Betty is singing, she taught her years ago before Betty could even walk. It goes, *Mary, Mary, quite contrary, how does your garden grow, with silver bells and cockle shells and pretty maids all in a row.*

She watches Betty place shells along the edges of the flower bed. Large scallop shells. "Now where did that child get those shells?" she says.

Betty has a supplier. It is Lenny. Once Lenny has moored the Nelly-May and sold his catch to the buyers he loads his latest haul of shells into a plastic FoodMart bag for the pretty little girl with the pink boots.

He usually leaves them by her garden gate, but this time she is in the lane to meet him. He stops the truck, smiles at her through his very whiskered chin and hands her the bag.

"Thank you mister," she says.

"You are welcome pretty lady," he says. "I'll try and get more for you in a few days, just look out for me."

Chapter 18

WHEN LENNY HITS the town he's just about on his last legs. He's managed to hitch a ride most of the way, but the last fifteen miles he walked. A truck driver had bought him a big mac yesterday. And a fisherman had bought him fish and chips the day before. "Are you looking for work young fella?" he'd asked Lenny.

"Yessir," Lenny had replied. "I may not look it, but I am strong."

The fisherman knew this without asking. He could see that the young man, or boy, had strength and stamina. "Be at the wharf next Tuesday by four in the morning and we'll give you a try," he'd said.

Lenny spent all Monday night on the wharf so as not to be late, plus he had nowhere to stay anyway. The fisherman, whose name Lenny learned, was Murray, handed him a floater jacket and special gloves and showed him what needed doing this first trip.

Lenny was a quick and eager learner, and before he knew it he was going out every day of the season catching lobster for the international market. The Nelly-May became his home. Unbeknown to Murray, Lenny sneaked back on when all had gone home each evening and slept in the wheelhouse. Clearing away all evidence before 4 am the next day.

For his hard work and dedication, Murray took him under his wing to a certain extent, and when he had to give up fishing for his rheumatism, he handed the boat over to Lenny. He also made sure Lenny was named in his will. The Nelly-May would be Lenny's.

Lenny did quite well for a few years, kept his nose clean, kept off the rum. He smoked to calm his nerves and one night he ran into Billy who quickly became his friend and confidant.

It was Billy who got Lenny started on the weed.

And it was the weed that began Lenny's inevitable fall. He began missing days out fishing. Days and days at a time. Sometimes weeks. He didn't know where the time went. He had lost it. He still had nowhere really to live until Billy offered him a place to stay. And that caused Lenny to stop going to the boat day in day out as he'd been so keen to do in the early days.

Chapter 19

"HERE YOU ARE again pretty lady," he says to Betty. She is standing on the wharf near his mooring as he brings in the Nelly-May. He throws her the mooring rope and she tries to heave it over to the rusting cleat. He laughs and hops out of the boat. "Like this," he shows her how to loop the rope and secure the boat. "What can I do for you pretty lady?" he says.

"Have you forgotten about the puppies?" she says.

He hasn't forgotten his promise to take her to see fictitious puppies. How he wishes he hadn't used that line. How he wishes he could just be normal with this sweet little girl. How he wishes things were different…

"Let me get my truck," he says. "Wait for me by the highway up there." Lenny doesn't want anyone to see him let Betty into his truck. He has a good idea what people might think. And he knows that in some respects they are probably so very right.

She knows how to climb into a truck. She knows where to find the hand holds and the foot holds. She pushes aside the old newspapers that cover the bench seat. She opens her bag.

"What have you got there," he says.

"It's my knitting for school," she says, "I'm knitting a pink sausage dog. I told you before, that's when you told me about the puppies."

"Shit, you're right," he says, then covers his mouth and grins. "Sorry," he says, "naughty word!"

"S'alright," she says, "Ma says it all the time."

Chapter 20

FRANNIE SITS IN a corner of the small restaurant on the side of the harbour. She sees the fishing boats coming in about midafternoon. She is bewildered by the hive of activity and doesn't remember it being at all like this from when she was here sixty years ago.

Then it was run down. Miserable. Nobody had a thing. Times were hard. The day she was raped called a halt to all her dreams. She told no-one. She didn't know the man who pulled her under the wharf and ravaged her until she passed out. Who held her down with one hand over her face while he ripped her body apart.

And then left after calling her a little slut who didn't even deserve that.

She told no-one. She knew nothing about life, about pregnancy, about her body. As she grew larger she just thought she was growing up quickly, getting fat like all the other women in the village. When her time came she hugged herself with what she thought was a bad belly ache, lay down in that old barn and gave birth.

It was like a nightmare from which she dearly needed to wake up. She ran, covered with blood from the birth of the baby. Frightened as a rabbit. She ran all day and all night until she hit the Salvation Army in a big town where no-one knew her. They took her in. Cleaned her up, fed her and made sure she was OK. She didn't tell them her name was Annie. "Frannie," she said. "Frannie Bennet."

They were good to her and helped her find work and somewhere to live.

Frannie looks down at the steaming cup of cappuccino that has been set before her in a dark green French coffee cup with a gold rim. Just like something she saw in an English movie recently. Then the little tiered cake stand, with assorted fancy cakes. Miniature iced sponge cakes, chocolate éclairs, cream horns, and blackberry tartlets. A little pot of clotted cream on the side with a silver soon.

As she looks up from this array of mouthwatering treats, she sees a tiny union jack flag in the corner of the restaurant's window. "Of course," she says, "it just has to be British, how on earth did the British find this forgotten corner of the planet?"

"By accident," came the reply. It turns out the owner is sitting at the next table having tea with a friend. "We saw the need, gave up the rat-race in Europe, and just, as they say, did it."

"Successful, yes?" says Frannie.

"More than we could have hoped," is the reply.

Frannie looks around, she sees every table is taken. It is around 4 o'clock when in England everything used to 'stop for tea'. She notices that the women are doing the ordering for the men. And it is the women who take their bank cards to the till on the way out and pay. The men are told to leave a tip.

"How things change," again she says aloud.

"Been here before?"

"I was born here," she says.

"We are doing a project on local history, would you like to stay a while and talk with us? Many folks have drifted away, we are trying to find out why."

"I'm not sure," says Frannie. She doesn't want to turn them down flat, she wonders if they may be able to help her find her boy. "I'm staying in town at The Best Western, just ask for Mrs. Lambert, that'll be enough to put you through. I do have a cell phone too, here's the number. But right now I am doing some personal research."

She leaves the restaurant with mixed feelings. She'd hoped to bump into a familiar name, or at least a descendent with a familiar name. She stands on the wharf and watches the boats tie up. One boat seems that it hasn't left the wharf in years, rusty and uncared for, the Nelly-May.

"Do you know whose boat this is?" she asks a small boy.

"That's old Lenny's boat, he's gone now."

Frannie doesn't reply, she knows what the small boy means.

"Ask Billy. He's always in the tavern. He'll tell you all about Lenny."

The tavern is in the centre of the community. Bicycles lean against the peeling painted wall. She can hear the guffaws of beery men within. Beery guffawing men don't bother Frannie. She can deal with them.

She's wearing a smart black worsted skirt suit with a faux mink stole around her shoulders. She has on black velvet ballet style shoes and a matching handbag with a gold link chain handle.

Her hair is coifed into a French twist and a gold clasp holds it in place. Slightly made up, she is still quite the beauty at 75.

The clamouring talk stops as Frannie enters the tavern.

Red nosed faces turn to see who has just entered. Men push back the beaks of their ball caps to see her a little better through the tavern's gloom.

A wolf whistle comes from the far corner. It is Billy.

"A gin and tonic," she says, "please."

"Ice and lemon?"

"No thank you."

"I'll bring it over if you'd like to take a seat."

Frannie looks for the cleanest table, the one with the least amount of stains, and the bench with the fewest crumbs.

Billy is the one with the curiosity. He picks up his beer bottle, wipes the froth from his top lip and saunters, in a way that a chubby sixty-year-old can saunter, over to the table. 'May I?" he says, all polite like.

"Please do," she says, "I'm Frannie."

"Howdy, fine lady," he says, remembering how Lenny called all females 'pretty lady' and making him swallow hard with the memory of his dear friend.

"I'm here to find out about someone," she says.

"Oh yeah," says Billy, not as a question, more as a concern. Wondering what he might have done, and if this was someone from the council. Although she looked old, surely not still working for the government. But you could never tell, could you?

"Yes," she says. "I'm looking for a guy called Billy."

Billy turns to stone. Has he been found out? But found out for what? His conscience obviously was playing snooker-balls in his pockets at this very moment.

"Are you Billy?" she says.

"I s'pose I'd better come clean," he says, "I sure am Billy as everyone here will tell ya."

"Oh good," says Frannie, "I thought you were. I understand you knew my son."

The tavern goes deathly quiet. You could hear the birds sing outside, a rare moment indeed in this tavern.

"If you mean Lenny, yes," says Billy, lowering his voice, solemnly looking at his friends at the bar, trying not to let the tear that he knew would come, roll down his cheek. He can feel his nose prickle like it did if he cried, when his nose would run down over his top lip and into his mouth.

"What can you tell me?" she says.

"I'm so, so sorry," says Billy. "Lenny died."

As Billy reaches for his drink, ash drops from his cigarette on to Frannie's black skirt. Frannie doesn't notice. She was still coming to terms with the bombshell. It seems more real now she is in the company of someone who knew her son.

"I'll take you to the grave if you like," he says.

"My son has a grave? Should I take flowers?"

"He'd like that," says Billy.

"Give me one of those," she says. "Please."

Frannie pulls hard on the cigarette. Breathes deeply and closes her eyes. "I should have come here sooner," she says, dropping her ash too, on her black skirt.

"He'd have liked that," says Billy.

"What else can I take?" she says.

"A beer," says Billy. "He always liked a beer."

They stand over her son's grave. "I should have loved you more," she says, gently pouring the beer over the earth.

"He'd have liked that," says Billy.

"Who's this?" She looks closer at the headstone next to Lenny. She recognises the names from the only clue, the slip of paper, she had a while back.

"Oh, that's ole Gordie and Ada, died a long time back. Fifty years or more. That's their old farm over there."

Frannie shields her eyes and looks over the fields at the crumbling farmhouse, "Nobody living there?"

"No," says Billy, "they had no family, it's bin for sale forever."

Chapter 21

LENNY FOLLOWS THE little girl. He likes her and he reckons she likes him more now, especially now she knows he likes puppy dogs too.

He sees her pink rubber boots bounce up and down, up and down along the muddy ruts in the lane. Her mother had waved her off at the garden gate, given her a small basket and a five-dollar bill and told her to come straight home with the bread.

Lenny knows it's Betty and that she is ten years old, small for her age, but sharp as a thumb tack Lenny hears. 'She must be clever if she can go shopping for bread,' he tells himself.

She stops at the end of the land, looks left and right. Then sees the daisies growing along the edge, she begins to pick the flowers, their little white petals surrounding the golden centres. 'Picking them for her ma, I guess,' says Lenny to himself, 'oh how I would have loved to pick flowers for my ma, if only I knew where she went, where she is, I could give her a flower and she would kiss my forehead and make the bad bad headaches go away.'

Betty sees Lenny then, "Hi," she says.

"Hi back atcha," says Lenny trying to be cool.

"Did you get the puppies?" she says.

"Not yet," he says, "but I know where they are, I c'n take ya."

"I'm not allowed to go far today," she tells him, "Ma sent me for the bread, then I must go straight home."

"Huh," says Lenny, "maybe some other time then."

Betty's mouth turns down at the corners, he thinks she is going to cry.

"Don't cry pretty lady," he says, "you'll spoil your pretty little face."

Betty perks up then, "'Nother day then?"

"Sure," he says, come find me at the wharf tomorrow after school."

"I will if it doesn't rain," she says. "'bout four o'clock? But I must be home for supper and to do my homework."

Chapter 22

FRANNIE SITS DOWN in the muddy grass beside Lenny's grave. "There is supposed to be a headstone," says Billy, "but it isn't made yet."

"You?" says Frannie.

"Yes, of course," says Billy. "Lenny was my bestest friend in the whole world."

"I'm glad he had you for a friend," she says. "That gives me some comfort. What kind of a life did he have?"

Billy does his best to disguise the fact that Lenny actually had a pretty miserable life. "He changed when he got the boat," he says. Billy closes his eyes. He shivers.

"Come on, let's go and get warm," says Frannie, "and let's get you some better clothes and a good meal in your belly. It's the least I can do after what you've done for my boy."

Billy is embarrassed but lets himself be drawn in by this old but elegant woman, with her fine gold rings and her rich woollen coat. With her earrings that sparkle like early morning frost on the grass behind his welfare apartment.

She smiles at him, "Don't be scared, I won't eat you."

Billy laughs then, "Lenny always said that," he says. "Quite a lot actually."

"It's no use us being miserable over what might have been," she says, "so let's look to the future. I'd like for you to come home with me, I have a big home. If that's what you'd like."

Chapter 23

BETTY PULLS LENNY by the hand. They climb up the lane to the top of the knoll. He follows like a dutiful child, letting Betty take over, as if she has suddenly become a mother to him. He wishes Billy were there too, so that they could see the view all together. Like a family. Like a Mother a Father and a little boy Lenny.

There is a large granite rock at the top. It is shaped like a scoop of ice cream that's had a bite taken out of it leaving an overhang, a sheltered place.

Betty has arranged a dolly's tea set in pink with flowers around the rims of all the cups and the saucers too. She has them laid out on an old raggy tea towel for a tablecloth.

"Sit down," she says.

Lenny is surprised at her bossy little squeaky voice. She had been so meek and docile down on the wharf, wheedling at him to take her to see the puppies. Now the little minx was squinting her eyes at him as if hypnotising him.

He watches carefully as she pulls her knitting out of her bag. He wonders what else she might have.

"Ya got a biscuit in there too?" he says.

"Only if you're good," she says. Smiling in a sneery way, showing a row of tiny white teeth.

"Oh, I'm always good," he says.

"Show me then."

He is unsure what she means. Does she want him to tidy the little she-cave she's made? Or does she want him to tell her a story or something? He decides the story is the best way forward and begins:

"There was once a little puppy called Elsa."

"That's a funny name for a puppy," she says.

"There was once a lion called Elsa," he says, "that's not in the story, that's true."

"OK."

He begins again, "There was once a little golden puppy called Elsa, her mistress called her Elsa after a lion, a real lion also called Elsa who lived in Africa, in the jungle."

"That's more like it," says Betty. "You are getting close to being good."

Lenny feels that age old quiver between his legs, low in his belly and he really is hoping it will go away soon. It seems the bossier and stricter the little pretty girl gets, the more it arouses him. He doesn't want to spoil anything. He just wants a biscuit really.

'She's such a pretty little thing,' he thinks, 'to look at anyway, but she seems to have turned nasty on me.' "So Elsa goes to live with a little girl with pink boots. The little girl is good at knitting and decides she will make a coat for Elsa. She gets her friend Lenny to take her to town to the yarn store in his truck. Together they choose the colours of the rainbow for the doggy coat: red, orange, yellow, green, blue, indigo and violet…"

"What's indigo?" she says.

"Indigo. It's a greyish blue colour, the colour of the clouds over there. You know we should probably head back now, it looks like rain on its way."

"You are going nowhere yet," she says.

Lenny is struck dumb and begins to stand, first on his hands and knees. Before he can get himself upright she is onto him. Stabbing at him with her knitting needles. In his face. In his eyes. In his throat.

"I know you," she says. "People like you. Dirty old men like to mess with kids like me. I've seen stuff on TV. You're supposed to know better. You're supposed to help us kids."

Her stabbing is frenzied. Over and over until she is out of strength and out of breath. Until she collapses on the side wall of the granite shelter. Her dolly's tea set strewn across the ground, some pieces have tumbled part way down the hill.

She looks down at what is left of the man she has been talking to. In disbelief she tries to pull out her knitting needles.

"Now I won't be able to finish my sausage dog," she says before fainting back, hitting her head on the rocks.

Chapter 24

WHEN THE SEARCH party finds Betty, she is comatose against the rock. If Billy hadn't spotted the dolly's tea cup in the dark they may not have found her before morning. By then hypothermia would be set in.

It was too late for Lenny, he had bled out from his jugular, probably only took minutes for him to die. What he could see through the one eye still functioning was anyone's guess.

But he would have seen little Betty revert to her normal sweetness having no idea of what she'd done.

It was too far off the road for an ambulance to bring back either of them. Betty's mother carried her in her arms to the bottom of the lane where the ambulance waited. Forensics soon arrived and after an initial examination, Lenny's body was carried out on a stretcher. Yellow police tape was run around the entire area as far as one of the dolly's teaspoons had rolled.

Chapter 25

BILLY DOESN'T TELL Frannie all of this, he really doesn't fancy reliving the entire trauma. He found them both. The little girl in the pink boots and his oldest and best friend together. He'd scratched his head later completely confused as to what they might have been doing there.

Lenny's pants were halfway down his legs. His flaccid dead penis shrivelled like a walnut, no, an almond more like. Billy zipped up Lenny's pants, he thought it inappropriate that anyone else should see. And he smoothed down the little girl's clothes too. If that was tampering with a crime scene he couldn't help that. It was the right thing for Billy to do. For both of them.

In the end, 'misadventure' was the conclusion. No-one could talk to Betty. She just wouldn't open her little red rosebud mouth for any authority. When she did it was to ask for her knitting.

"I'll get you some new knitting started," said her mother.

But Betty declined that, she wanted the knitting needles Miss Watson had given to her, and the pink wool. Miss Watson visited every afternoon after school was out. She talked to Betty, or just sat with her. She went over the lessons the class had had that day.

Betty looked through her, to the wall and window beyond, to the view of the hill where it had all happened. Then, "Where is Elsa?' she said.

"Who is Elsa?" says Miss Watson.

"Elsa is a puppy dog, a golden-haired puppy dog. The man. The man Lenny was taking me to see puppy dogs. Elsa was to be mine."

Miss Watson repeated this to Betty's mother as they sat round the kitchen table drinking coffee later. Betty's mother just shook her head. "She's delirious," she said. "It doesn't make any sense. Lenny, you say? Not that Lenny?"

"He is, sorry was, the man she was with. The man who died," says Miss Watson.

Betty's mother is beside herself, "I told her not to go off anywhere, I told her not to talk to strangers. Do you think she will ever be OK?"

"I hope so," says Miss Watson, "but I think it will take some time, we will just have to be patient."

"I never really knew him," says Betty's mother. "Do you know any more?"

"Not a lot. He was a buddy of Billy Mac. He had a boat, the Nelly-May, so a fisherman I guess. Some say he was born here in a barn and was taken and put into care by social services, but it is only gossip.

Chapter 26

FRANNIE PUTS A notice in the newspaper. It is Lenny's obituary:

Leonard Francis. Died September 14th of unnatural causes aged sixty years.

Son of Frances Catherine Lambert originally of Hellings Cove. Best friend to Billy also of Hellings Cove.

'Unloved in life, now loved in death, no time for regrets'

Chapter 27

EVERYONE IN THE coffee shop has the paper open to the obits pages. "Who is this Frances Catherine Lambert?" they ask each other.

Of course the moment Billy waltzes in through the doors, letting in an icy blast, they are on him. "Who is she?"

"That's his ma," he says. "She'd come looking for 'im. Didn't know he was dead or nuffin'. I don't think. Just too bad. Just too late. Poor Lenny."

Billy doesn't tell them that she's offered to take him back with her. He doesn't know what to do, whether to just leave quietly without a fuss. What? Without Lenny there is nothing for him now in Hellings Cove. "She is going to sell the boat though, or maybe just give it away."

They want to know how to get in touch with her. Billy says, "I'll give her your messages if that's OK."

He has suddenly become quite an entity in the community, almost celebrity status. People clamouring around him like he's a superstar or something. A cup of coffee, double double and a Boston Cream doughnut is put in his hand without him ordering.

"This is just plain embarrassing," he says, "but thanks a lot, much appreciated." With that he swings out of the coffee shop and heads off down the road towards the hotel.

"That's where she must be staying," the cry goes out and at least a dozen people pour out onto the freezing cold street and head to the Best Western.

The staff at the hotel are non-committal about who is staying where. The guys are too late to see Billy disappearing into the elevator and pressing 4 for the fourth floor. For a while they sit around in the hotel foyer in the hopes that at least Billy or the woman will appear. But no luck. Eventually they drift off, "It's my supper time," they say to each other.

As the last of them slip out through the main revolving glass doors, the hotel receptionist calls Frannie in her room. "They've all gone," she says. "But I'd give it half an hour, if you like I'll ask your car to be brought to the side exit."

Billy sits stiffly in a new pair of jeans with a plaid shirt and a leather jacket. Frannie says, "We'll get you a decent haircut and some more stuff when we get home." Billy shivers.

Frannie has noticed his discomfort about everything in the hotel, how he wasn't sure about which spoon to use for his soup, how she knew he really needed to pass gas and went red in the face to stop himself. How he sits on the edge of his chair as if about to bolt. She wonders if taking him with her will work.

"You don't have to come," she says. "There's always Lenny's boat, we could get it fixed up."

Frannie sees Billy's eyes light up. How he takes a deep breath and sits back n the chair. She's also thinking about the visit to the Real Estate office earlier in the day, and her offer on Gordie and Ada's ruined farmhouse.

About the Author

S.B. Borgersen is a British/Canadian author, of middle England and Hebridean ancestry, whose favoured genres are flash and micro fiction, and poetry.

Sue was educated at diverse institutions including boarding at a French convent in Nicosia, Cyprus before transferring in 1958 to a boarding school for military brats where she published her first story, <u>My Life Story: told by Laika, the Sputnik Dog</u> in *The Crusader*, the first magazine of King Richard School, Dhekelia, Cyprus.

Sometime after that was the freedom of The North Warwickshire School of Art.

She had a diverse career path, an analyst in a shoe factory, the same thing for a children's book publisher, teaching art, and filing for the civil service, but mostly she climbed a precarious ladder in the IT industry culminating in strategy and project management, which, by necessity in those days, included writing writing writing mountains of non-fiction — always allowing herself to be slightly creative with proposals, reports, technical and training documentation.

Sue turned her back on industry and commerce in the early nineties, escaping the stressful rat-race and finding the simple life and peaceful place she'd always sought to allow for creativity. That place was Nova Scotia where she returned to her skills from art school and made an uncomplicated living as a visual artist and potter. That is, until she got the creative writing bug.

Since 2000 her writing has won prizes, been mentioned in Hansard and published internationally in literary journals and anthologies (print and online). The list of publications is extensive and can be found at www.sueborgersen.com

She is a loyal member of The Writers' Federation of Nova Scotia and an enthusiastic member of the international online writers' group for expats, Writers Abroad.

Sue lives in a crumbling old house on the shores of Nova Scotia with her patient husband and a clutch of lovable rowdy dogs. She has two middle-aged children.

S.B. Borgersen writes every day.

Lightning Source UK Ltd.
Milton Keynes UK
UKHW011043140421
381978UK00002B/329